A LETTER TO MOTHER

FROM DESTRUCTION TO CONSTRUCTION

A LETTER TO MOTHER

FROM DESTRUCTION TO CONSTRUCTION

ARUP MITRA

ATLANTIC PUBLISHERS AND DISTRIBUTORS

Published by
ATLANTIC PUBLISHERS AND DISTRIBUTORS
B-2, Vishal Enclave, Opp. Rajouri Garden, New Delhi-27
Phones : 5413460, 5429987, 5466842

Sales Office
4215/1, Ansari Road, Darya Ganj, New Delhi-110 002
Phones : 3273880, 3285873, 3280451
Fax : 91-11-3285873
web : www.atlanticbooks.com
e-mail : info@atlanticbooks.com

ISBN 81-269-0146-2

Typeset at
APD Computer Graphics, Delhi

Printed in India at
Nice Printing Press, Delhi

DEDICATED TO

"Full many a gem of purest ray serene,

In the dark unfathomed caves of ocean bear :

Full many a flower is born to blush unseen

And waste its sweetness in the desert air."

(Thomas Gray)

ACKNOWLEDGMENTS

This work had the privilege of receiving suggestions on both analytical issues and stylistic presentation from Ms. Gopa Das and Dr. Indrani Gupta. Ms. Vandana Preyashi offered detailed comments and extensive editorial support with great generosity. In depth discussions with my sister Ms. Rina Chanda helped enrich the contents in some of the sensitive parts in the text. Dr. Deb Kusum Das offered useful insights to the incidents narrated in the text. Dr. Ayodhya Das and Ms. Soudamini Das encouraged me immensely to go ahead with this project. I am grateful to all of them.

Finally, I remember my parents, who inculcated the ability to do a careful analysis of characters without falling into the domains of mere gossip — the tendency implanted in human nature. A story emerges from the heart of a gossip only when it develops the power to relate an individual case study to multitudes, and manifests an element of timelessness in itself.

ARUP MITRA

FAMILY TREE

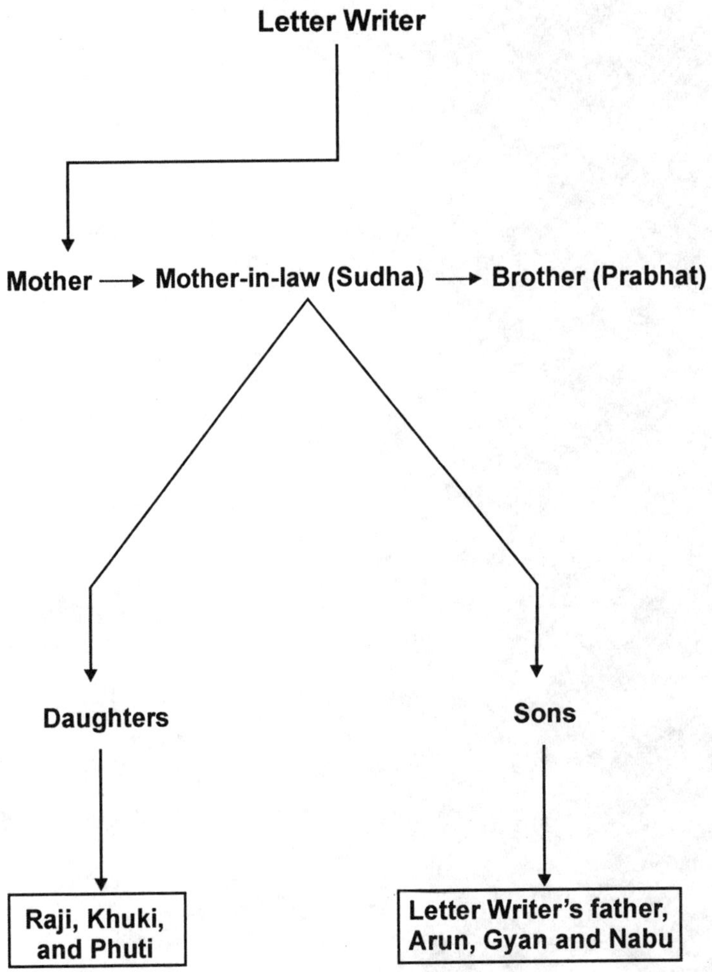
Letter Writer
Mother
Mother-in-law (Sudha)
Brother (Prabhat)
Daughters
Sons
Raji, Khuki, and Phuti
Letter Writer's father, Arun, Gyan and Nabu

My Dear Ma,

To watch the star-studded sky hanging on my head like a veil has been the dream of my life. A little peace, a little equanimity — that is all I have always wanted. No, I never wished to run away from life, and become a recluse. I have always wanted to enjoy life like an ordinary human being. But too much of involvement can never hold any charm. It is just the balance between the two — involvement and indifference — that I wanted to maintain and, therefore, I made every possible effort to keep the light of my love for nature, ignited even in the midst of my most pre-occupied days. But this was not somehow acceptable to your mother-in-law or sisters-in-law. They always mistook this attitude of mine for madness. Their strong comments did hurt me a lot but I never took them to my heart.

During my childhood, your in-laws, particularly the elder sister-in-law, wanted me to gossip with her in my leisure. But I was bent on utilising my time in the most productive way that I could. Constant introspection and contemplation upon myself and beyond, gave me insurmountable pleasure and peace. I am sure you understand what I mean. After all I inherited this quality from you — you who had encountered similar difficulties when you stepped into this house after your marriage.

My journey — journey to self-sufficiency — started there on, my aim being to cultivate my capabilities. Since my adolescence days, I did not want to depend on any one — financially or emotionally. I was determined to venture alone into the ocean of uncertainty in search of self-respect.

Do you remember, how your mother-in-law, Sudha and sister-in-law, Raji once brought false allegation against you? I was too young at that time to understand the complexities of human character. Every morning it was your duty to sweep grandmother's room. The maid, who possibly came from a low-caste family, was not allowed to enter her room. So if you somehow could not clean it, grandma herself would begin the work to leave it incomplete. One morning your sister-in-law, Raji, alleged that some coins were missing from her purse which she had kept in grandma's room. Grandma joined her shortly, and soon the entire family was made to realise that their daughter-in-law was the biggest thief that the world could have ever produced. Your mother, your father and all your forefathers were dragged into the picture. Their character was assassinated to the best possible extent and to the maximum satisfaction of your in-laws. Mother, I remember how miserable you felt. I know, you could never have done such an act. You said nothing, only tears rolled down your cheek. I, as a child, thought the earth should break into two pieces, the sky should speak aloud in favour of your innocence. But no such thing happened and we had to live in disgrace and dismay. No one came to your rescue; you faced the '*agni-parikhya*' all by yourself. And you kept burning in the fire of shame, dishonour and humiliation. You were sobbing constantly all through the night. Lying next to you I could feel your heart beat within me.

It was Wednesday I still remember, you were getting ready to take us for Bubu's wedding. Father did not like attending social functions, and grandmother insisted that we should attend the function else her brother, Prabhat, would never forgive her. After all, it was his eldest daughter's wedding. Raji could not suppress her wrath and jealousy any more. She thought she would be asked to carry the family gift to Prabhat's house. But grandma knew that Raji's presence in her brother's house would create only chaos. Prabhat's wife Tanima would not like to see her husband flirting with Raji in front of the visitors. And Raji's shameless reciprocations in a hoarse (but trying to be seductive) voice would be unbearable to Tanima. But you had to bear the brunt of grandma's decision; one large portion of your *benarasi* which you had just taken out from the cupboard, was spoilt by a scissor. In fact, she stole several of your saris from your trunk but you kept quiet every time in order to avoid unpleasantness in family. But this one, which she mercilessly snipped, was presented by your mother to you on your wedding to wear in the 'first night'. I could not understand at that time what it meant to you. Today I understand its significance, and it hurts to recall the incident. Hats off to your patience, you wept for a while sitting in the dark corner of the roof, and later recollected yourself and smilingly held my hands and took leave of grandma to attend the marriage.

Next day Raji added some powder in your tea. I saw it myself but before I could tell you she put me to some work. When I returned, you had already drunk it. God alone knows, how much you suffered from stomach-ache! What a sadistic pleasure Raji derived from seeing you groaning in pain.

Prabhat came to visit her sister and beloved niece the next evening. All these days he had a very hectic schedule. The departure of the newly wed couple enabled him to come back to his regular place of relaxation. It amused him to hear that you were unwell because of overeating! "Daughters-in-law are supposed to be shy; shyness is the ornament of women. These days they have lost all humility. Given an opportunity they would eat with both the hands." Raji joined the dialogue very eagerly, and once again you died with shame.

Grandfather got for you the garland from the Gopalji temple, which was offered to the deity, and he enjoyed seeing you tie it in your hair. Prabhat, as usual, walked in at 9.00 p.m. sharp and kept staring at you with all evil shadows in his eyes. I felt like pricking his eye-balls. You did notice it and quickly left the room. No sooner did you leave than I heard him making a pass at you. With great enthusiasm of having discovered the most rare element in the world he turned to his sister and niece, "your daughter-in-law seems to be still enjoying sex with her husband. Children are grown-up; high time, she must refrain from all this." I am sure, Mother, you had heard it. It must have absolutely shaken and wrecked you. You still did not utter a single word. I, as a child of eight, could only follow some bit of it but did not have the guts to raise my voice. I wish you had told father. No, that would not have helped, as you did rightly. It would have only created further complicacies. In the absence of father the intensity of your torture would have only increased.

Guests had come. You were asked to serve them tea. After one sip Raji quickly commented, "Oh it tastes like the urine of the horse." Mother, why did you keep quiet? You should have given her a befitting reply, "How many times have you tasted the urine?" But you would then say, "generous neglect." Several times you prepared delicious dishes, and guests would appreciate a lot. All this while Sudha and Raji would be dying with suppressed anger, which I, a child, could notice.

One of the lady visitors was concerned about your skeletal figure : "Sudha don't you feed your daughter-in-law properly?" In reply both your mother-in-law and sister-in-law replied,

"Her mother did not feed her adequately. In growing age children need to be given protein diet. Our daughter-in-law's mother was busy in conceiving one after another. She did not have any time for this unfortunate one." Disgrace must have killed your soul but still you put your head down and walked out quietly.

All these incidents prevail upon my mind every moment. I keep wondering, how can a human being attain development of the inner self in the midst of this torture. You were not financially independent — rather not allowed to be so, in spite of your qualification. How many post-graduates in English were produced in mid-fifties? I am sure, you would have got a job had you tried a little. But father would never want any compromise with his comforts. In-laws would be horrified by the idea that the eldest daughter-in-law of this great Mitra dynasty would go out to work. And you always wanted peace so you did not annoy anyone. But, mother, letting others live in peace does not necessarily mean you too can be in peace. Some do not deserve peace. If you let them enjoy it, they cultivate their energy to trouble you. Best thing is to put them into tension, so that their energies are diverted elsewhere. But you always took this attitude to be childish, and explained us the greatness of piety.

After this digression I get back to what I was saying. If you were financially independent you could have at least walked out of the house and led a peaceful life. Perhaps, we might not have got the protection we enjoyed in our father's house. But then who cares! Peace is much more precious than comforts.

When everything is gone, nature continues to remain. You had enormous faith in nature. I know how much pleasure you derived after spending an hour on the roof looking at the sky. What an outlet you sought for yourself! At the end of the day's hard work you would run to the terrace to watch the sun-set and would keep waiting till you located your familiar stars in the sky. Any unpleasantness in the family and you would quickly go to the terrace to be alone. After a while you always looked rejuvenated — as if nothing had happened. Nature provided you the energy required to face the turmoil of life.

You never wore gorgeous or expensive clothes. Neither you nor your in-laws, particularly the ladies, liked them. You did not like them perhaps because your upbringing was different. But for others the reason was quiet different. Our youngest aunt Phuti lost her husband at a young age and she and her two sons were dependent on us. Although she continued to stay in her in-laws house, help, both in kind and cash, was remitted regularly. Grandma would constantly compare and contrast our way of living with theirs. As a result, you decided to give up using whatever little treasure you had. Father would neglect us intentionally in order to avoid the comments of grandma that Phuti and her sons were in deep misery but the truth is that due to everyone's sympathy, Phuti and her sons led the most luxurious life. They got the best possible clothing and every fashionable item of the time. This is exactly what her in-laws were saying once though Phuti retorted angrily, "It is their sheer jealousy." We, on the other hand, did not have anything better than the ordinary stuff. We never objected, for you taught us that hardships make one successful.

Only for the name sake you were the wife of a Neurologist and we, his children. You led a most ordinary life, even going to the extent of remaining underfed at several occasions. The outcome was that you and your children always looked like skeletons. In midst of affluence we knew only misery. Every statement of grandma made a reference to Phuti's destiny and struggle, and in comparison to that we were said to be lucky. If her sons were unwell we were to be blamed. Our fault was that we did not fall sick. God was said to be partial, unkind to Phuti and unduly gracious to us. Every time father would get some tonic for us, grandma would begin her commentary about Phuti's misery. Father would then decide to send them to Phuti's sons. I am shocked that Phuti never objected to this. Only now I can sense her extracting attitude.

One constant accusation was that you and your children were constantly jealous of Phuti's sons. As a child when I asked you, innocently, to explain all this, you kept quiet. But today I feel, you should have told us bluntly that jealous were your in-laws of us, not we of them. And it is the nature of the human mind to visualise the rest of the world as it exists within oneself. He who suffers from jaundice sees the whole world yellow. But you did not want to pollute our mind by criticising our elders. I wonder whether your approach was wrong, because you can't imagine how much I have suffered from these filthy untrue comments. Sometimes I actually believed what others had to say — that we were really jealous of others, otherwise why would they say it all the time. And at that age it was but natural on my part to think so. Your clarifications could have made me happy and confident of myself.

Grandma and Raji wished you death, and us, physical and mental disabilities. But these wishes never came true. If bad wishes were to rule, the devils would have driven the universe chaos. They always conspired against us and never wanted that we should come to know about it. That was probably the reason why you were always discouraged to make friends in the neighbourhood. Aunt Bulu and aunt Manu respected and admired you. Aunt Manu being our nearest neighbour would try to chat with you every evening on the terrace. Joba and her other sisters would assemble with their mother, Manu on their terrace and we would accompany you to ours. Then both the ladies would open up the entire stock of their memories of a bygone era. Sometimes we enjoyed your chat, and sometimes we were asked to move away towards another corner of the terrace if it involved some episodes of romantic relationships of some of your acquaintances. Nevertheless our relaxation revolved around your topics of conversation. In order to keep a track of your conversation grandma would at least a dozen times pay visits to the open space below the terrace in the pretext of watering the plants. Interestingly, Raji's prayer time coincided with your time of chit-chat. She would constantly come closer to the window under the pretext of offering incense to the photographs of gods and goddesses. Even as a child I could see both curiosity and anger in her eyes. Why were you socialising with outsiders? Then I could not understand the cause of her disapproval. Later on, I realised that your socialisation with other aunts held the possibilities of you being made aware of drawbacks of your in-laws. Secondly, and more importantly, when a crisis would come, there should not be any one for you to fall back on. And the crisis? They were planning it every day bit by bit, placing one brick after another.

The day you and aunt Manu would be laughing a lot over some episode of your childhood days, Raji and grandma would begin great sermons as soon as father would return from the clinic in the late evening. They would reflect upon how mean and lowly aunt Manu's background had been. What acts of shrewdness she had performed when she came as a daughter-in-law to the Mitra family and so on. The primary objective was to convey you, through father that your socialisation was disapproved by the royal committee, and hence it would be desirable not to proceed further. Father, without trying to realise the actual reason, would endorsed the views of his mother and sister. However, he never forced you to implement them. You, therefore, did not give up your friendship with other aunts in the neighbourhood.

The same thing was repeated in our case. Whenever Didi's friends visited us, grandma would reflect on their parents' character, their background and their forefathers' misdeeds. If Sunanda's grandma, Murala, and all her daughters had a love-marriage what had Didi's friendship with Sunanda got to do with it? Several times Sunanda heard grandma grumbling at her, and she did feel bad about it. Overtly the advice of grandma and Raji was out of deep concern — for our character building — yet, I could feel even at that tender age that somewhere something was grossly wrong — that their intensions were perfectly evil, though suppressed. Real concern never believes in domination, and genuineness is always straight, for it cannot follow a crooked path.

Your mother and sister wanted to pay us a visit for a few days. They were coming all the way from Nagpur to have a '*darshan*' of Lord Jaganath. Puri is hardly 100 km from Cuttack, and it was quite natural for your mother to expect that she would come and stay with her daughter and that her son-in-law would take her to Puri for a day. But who would reveal this to our grandma for approval. After all, she was the boss of the family, the Prime Minister of the household, holding specifically the portfolios of finance and home. Raji, of course, held special power.

Being totally shaken by the thought that grandma would pounce on you on hearing the news of your mother's arrival, you persuaded father to break the news. He avoided it coolly. In desperation you turned to me. I was too young to understand your fear — the fear of being humiliated in front of everyone — including the servants and maids. However, when you cajoled me repeatedly I did go up to grandma to unravel the facts. "Who's coming? Why? Is this a hotel?" She retorted. I felt so helpless. Even as a child I could imagine how sad you would feel on learning about her reaction. I kept on combing her hair, put powder on her face, massaged her feet with coconut oil so that she would calm down a little and grant the permission. Well, grandma loved flattery and it worked on her. Quickly she calmed down and settled the agreement for three days' stay. I jumped with joy and ran to the kitchen to inform you. Your mother's visit was, after all, like a shower of spring flower from the Heaven for us. In fact, how many times did we meet her in our entire lifetime? Hardly thrice or so. Father was surprised to note that the bill was passed in the parliament without much hue and cry.

But our joy was threatened in the evening when Prabhat joined Raji's Pandemonium, where efforts were initiated to sabotage our small joys in life. But uncle Arun came over to our side, and thus their plans failed miserably. I loved uncle Arun for his straight forwardness, his blunt support for justice and his respect for truth, how so ever unpleasant it could be. Being a bachelor he loved his mother more than anyone, but if he were to select one between the two — mother and truth — he preferred to cast in favour of the latter. Perhaps, this is the reason why you also respected uncle Arun all through your life. Grandma was extremely scared of him. Even Raji would not dare to say anything on his face. Prabhat was a crook and he understood the gravity of command that Arun had in the house. He would not, therefore, dare to conspire and spoil something, which Arun had agreed to.

I felt that day that if you were financially independent then you need not have to cut such a sorry figure. You never had any money at your disposal? Your in-laws didn't let you work, they didn't allow you to run the household, and even for pocket money they always impressed upon father to give you none. They derived a sadistic pleasure by watching you penniless, by making you feel helpless in situations that could make anyone's existence impossible. To put it in short, they made sure that you should not be able to walk out of the house if your sufferings cross all limits. Within the same household Raji was allowed to work but not you. So, the rule was not merely women-specific; there was a big discrimination between the daughter and the daughter-in-law.

But why did father listen to them so obediently? Why didn't he realise that you shouldn't be begging for your personal expenses? Sometimes, when he would refuse to give you any money, how overwhelmed did Raji look with joy! How sarcastically did your mother-in-law laugh at you! They wanted to bring all kinds of misery to you. And wished that you should feel miserable. Daughters-in-law should remain depressed, then only she would be obedient. Happiness of the daughter-in-law in their dictionary meant arrogance, which should be eliminated by all means. But you intelligently always tried not to feel miserable about your misery.

I tell you mother, without money a person is nothing; possesses no personality. Money is the biggest asset that empowers an individual both within and outside the family. Just getting enough to eat and live comfortably is not sufficient for a personality to develop. Whether you actually spend or not is a secondary question, the primary issue is the ability to spend. If you don't have command over resources, your status can be reduced or demeaned at anytime at the convenience of others, to that of a "thief," or a "beggar's daughter." Without that command I think even a queen is no better than a beggar. Despite heavy dowry, women in north India enjoy no status; as the dowry money goes to the in-laws. On the other hand, women in south have a greater role to play in the decision making process because they enjoy the entitlement to land, which remains in their ownership all through their life.

With the prompting of his mother, father used to exclaim, "what is the need for you to have money? Whatever you require is provided to you instantly." But I wish, he, for that matter every one in the world, particularly the men, would understand the difference between what one gets and what one can acquire oneself. You may not actually want to acquire anything but the feeling that one can get it as per one's wish, is something, I think, that holds the key to all freedom and liberty. And you were denied in all possible ways of the actual access to the path of freedom.

I remember, how you had to literally fall at father's feet to get the permission to visit your parents, which could be only once in three years. Father thought it was an unnecessary expenditure. But that was just a superficial explanation. He knew that in your absence there would be none to look after him. Particularly, when he would be returning from the hospital in the late afternoon, the entire household would be under the lull of day-slumber. Raji's and your mother-in-law's worry was that who would manage the kitchen. Grandma never had a knack for cooking, and Raji was too lazy to get even a glass of water for herself.

We had no source of entertainment, and very few joyous moments in our childhood as far as outing was concerned. So two days of journey in the train to Nagpur was something that we always looked forward to. Besides, the very thought that there would not be much studies to do, and in the evening maternal uncle and aunt would take us out for a stroll thrilled us infinitely.

As there was no direct train connecting Cuttack and Nagpur, you felt a little nervous about changing the train at Kharagpur all by yourself with two young children to be looked after. You expected one of our uncles to accompany us at least upto Kharagpur, but Raji and Prabhat would try their best to sabotage the idea. In the freshly awakened household one could hear Grandma's voice piercing through all the bricks of the walls, wishing desperately for the cancellation of our trip. We would run away to the top most terrace so that the first music of the dawn one could escape and save it for the rest of the day.

Uncle Gyan was the only exception in the family. I hardly ever saw him lose temper on trivial issues. In addition, he was impartial, detached and considerate. He offered to accompany you to Nagpur for your younger sister's wedding on finding father's inability to do so. Do you think your mother-in-law and Raji did not load him with unsolicited suggestions to dissuade him from travelling with you. But he had his own mind. To assert, one need not be rough. One can be cool, patient and yet firm.

When your other sisters visited Nagpur, they had adequate, if not a lot, to spend. But our case was different. Father always gave you only a little more than what would be required to book the return tickets. We were always running short of funds. Anyway I don't blame father for this because grandma and Raji would squeeze him to the extent of leaving just a few pennies in his hands. His usual contribution to the family would continue irrespective of whether we lived in Cuttack or not.

You were not allowed to mix with anyone and to cultivate friendship with others. This would smoothen the process of your exploitation by your in-laws, as none would be there to challenge them socially. Besides, it would enable them to spread their one-sided stories describing you as a worthless creature. Society is selfish; it never tries to understand the reasons even if one is really worthless. At all times society has accepted the gifts from the individuals, but when it comes to giving, it declares that it has nothing to offer; its hands are all empty. Some individuals in retaliation to this attitude of the society have discarded it and have taken to ascetic life, others have tried unsuccessfully to reform it and some have continued to suffer remaining squeezed beneath its wheels. I prefer the middle-path. It does not matter even if all our efforts are in vain. The fact that we retaliated and tried to change it without abandoning it, is a matter of great comfort and pride to me. Sometimes sincere efforts even though without success, bring us a lot of satisfaction. But virtuousness, which teaches not to challenge or prompts to escape the crisis, holds no meaning to me at all.

Your mother-in-law, Sudha, and sister-in-law, Raji made ceaseless efforts to frighten you in all possible ways, so that you remain subdued forever. You didn't have access to finance, you were not allowed to make friends, your relatives stayed far away and were not allowed to visit you — a perfect combination of all factors to create a fear-psychosis in you. In moments of domestic conflicts you had nowhere to escape. Your unflinching service to the household continued even when you were absolutely exhausted, and mentally in no position to give a single grain. But you consoled yourself by saying that this is how might has dominated in all times. You were scared if you went to Nagpur for a month, then your in-laws may impress upon father not to bring you back. On the other hand, what was the guarantee that your parents would welcome you back? You didn't have a job, so it was not possible to be on your own. Yes, you did think several times of committing suicide because you did mention a couple of times. Perhaps after uttering this, you imagined our misery in your absence, and thus gave up the idea of taking such an extreme step.

But your tolerant behaviour did not produce any result that can be considered to be good either for you or for them. I say it was not good for them because it could not bring a positive change in their behaviour. Sometimes, seeing the agony of the person whom one tortures, his/her heart melts, like what had happened to Asoka at the Kalinga War — transformed from being *Chandasoka* to *Dharmasoka*. But nothing happened to Raji or Raji's mother, or Prabhat.

We all kept wondering about Prabhat; years passed by yet the man did not cease to visit his sister and niece. The heavy downpour of July nights or the sultry heat of the summer was weaker than his determination. Illegitimate affairs are the most powerful missiles that can destroy several households simultaneously. Didn't he ever feel embarrassed to imagine what others might have been thinking about him? No, some characters, such as Sakuni in *Mahabharata*, are so wretched and thick-skinned that they don't get affected by others' sensitivity. Their insensitivity makes them grossly insensible.

Prabhat was, perhaps, determined to ruin our father's life

and career. Although he our father's uncle, it was strange that he had evil designs against father. Perhaps because of the narrow age gap between him and our father, he could not overcome the jealousy that originated from several factors. First of all, our father was intelligent and he pursued his career in Neurology despite financial constraints. Father's motivation and dedication made him attain success, and established him as a Professor at an early age. He did not earn much in his entire lifetime because of honesty and love for the poor. His fame, spread far and wide, knew no bound. Throughout his working life he remained the only Professor in Neurology in Orissa. On the other hand, Prabhat had pitiably managed to get through in the examinations. He was a sales tax lawyer, notorious for his dishonesty and ill-got money. And ill-got is always ill-spent. As he was a miser, ill-got money showed its repercussions on other characters. His son spent money as much as he could on drinks and drugs. Prabhat's wife, a simple lady, suffered from tremendous complex because of her huge structure. Prabhat had abandoned her long ago. He disliked her in spite of her dedicated service to all the members in the household. According to Prabhat, she was no match for him because she was only a matriculate, and was not intelligent. According to Raji, Prabhat was too good-looking a man in comparison to his fat wife. But, is physical charm everything in life? Does the inner quality of a person have no value? Her steady service to her husband, unfortunately had no recognition. She did every bit of the household work and also visited a vegetable market, which was unheard in your time in a small town like Cuttack. Since Prabhat suspected the integrity of every servant, and he himself had no time for such petty activities, his wife had accepted it as a part of her duty. Being the bread-earner he enjoyed all the luxury that a not-so-good-looking wife could provide even at the cost of her life, in order to get the slightest appreciation from her husband, not to talk of affection. He exploited his wife more and more, and increasingly became jealous of our father because he had got a qualified wife like you, obedient children and, over and above, his sky-touching fame. Not everyone can be talented, nor can all acquire fame. But with a slight effort one can be happy if one is a little rational in realising that they could have been deprived of what they have. But that is the tragedy of life, man overlooks the well in his own premises, and runs miles after miles to quench his thirst elsewhere. I don't mind what one does in his personal life as long as it does not affect others. But the moment it harms others, the issue does not remain merely personal morality, it becomes an issue concerning social welfare.

Prabhat's son took the full advantage of the strained relationship between his parents. By the time he was eighteen he had emerged as an anti-social element. This made Prabhat the most frustrated creature on earth. The day he suspected that we had grown suspicious of his relationship with Raji, he became determined to ruin us. His nephew, Tabu, told me about this only a few days back. One evening Tabu heard him telling someone, "Gopal's wife and children have become extremely proud. Therefore, we must teach them a lesson."

No matter how much education women have acquired, at the back of their mind the feeling of insecurity remains predominant. And this is mainly because the society is hostile towards them, particularly those who are single. So, by hook or by crook every woman has to get married, and if marriage does not provide a comfortable home, she has to make every effort, even sacrificing every little pleasure of her life — not to talk of her independence — to keep it going. This is mainly because she thinks that she has nowhere to go. Job might give her financial independence but it's difficult to find another home. As a divorcee she is not welcome by her parents or brothers, and this she knows very well. The day-to-day struggle and the agony that a single woman faces staying alone, is something that scares her from taking any decision for the sake of justice..She learns to live with injustice, compromising at every turn of the obstructive path of her life. Ultimately, she may succeed in withstanding all the misery in the household she has been married to, but at what cost? It is at the cost of her rationality, her intellect and her personality. She gets a home but intellectually she is reduced to a vegetable. Many of us, perhaps, realise this but still accept it because of insecurity. Mother, you also fell prey to this. You were educated, you could have walked out but whereto? At least initially you would have required some support. Your parents were far off; they, anyway, I am sure, would not have appreciated your stand. Your elder brothers, who could have helped you, were too selfish to undergo any loss of their comfort for your sake. So you decided in complete sanity to accept every torture of your in-laws like all other ninety per cent of the Indian women.

A constant fear prevailed upon your mind. If they drive you out what would happen? Where would you go? Suppose they pointed at your character and if father believed them, what would be your fate? The best thing you thought was not to tell father anything about the ill-treatment you got. This, you thought, would at least not create further misunderstanding and aggravate the situation. Your fear was, perhaps, imaginative. Father, I am sure, would not have believed them if they had said any such thing. But fear begets fear, and it has no bound. Particularly when one does not have the option of sharing it with anyone, the mind becomes the greatest enemy of oneself.

Your self-confidence constantly shaken, you increasingly felt that this household was your only heaven on earth. Your fear degenerated your strength, which, in turn made you more dependent on the very source of your fear. You entered a vicious circle. You absorbed everything, and so did you teach us. And this is what every woman does in our society.

As fear persisted in your mind, your power of concentration declined gradually. Your work left scope for criticism. Continuous criticism reduced your confidence further, and you committed more mistakes in your day-to-day activities. These minor slips were, of course, of no importance if we see today in retrospect with a wide vision in life, but to those who had nothing but to criticise others, pitfalls could offer more food for thought. You often forgot to dry your clothes. You would keep them in a corner of the terrace and would not spread them unless reminded of. And your critics always took this opportunity to characterise you as mentally imbalanced. Sometimes you became unmindful while cutting vegetables — in the middle of your job suddenly you would stop and start staring at the sky. Again your in-laws took the opportunity to make you a laughing-stock. You sometimes cooked curry, which was not enough for the entire household. Your scrutinisers called you inefficient, inefficiency stemming from inattentiveness, which was again attributed to madness.

One of your fears, which shook you absolutely, was due to your mother-in-law's and sister-in-law's concocted stories about your misbehaviour. They would narrate them to father as soon as he would return from work. They would all join hands to emphasise that you misbehaved with everyone as soon as father left home, whereas God alone knows, it was just the opposite. They alleged that you extended your undue support to us when they tried to correct our mistakes. You were cast as someone who taught her children to be impolite and arrogant; you instructed them to misbehave with all of their relatives. And the worst part was that father, at least temporarily, believed these stories. His immediate reaction was unbelievably scary. He would burst into anger and start scolding all of us in most offensive language. He did not care even if other people were present on the scene. Do you remember how Ravi, one of our young servants, once burst into laughter as soon as fathers' heavy downpour was over. Ravi imitated father and described the scene, "Babu today called Boudi non-sen (non-sense), idet (idiot), rachkal (rascal)." But I don't entirely blame father; any man returning home after attending innumerable patients for almost seven to eight hours continuously in the hospital would lose his temper to learn that his wife does not have even an ounce of respect for elders, or patience to follow their suggestions. One great quality of father was that he would soon realise the game plan of his relatives soon after he had had a shower, and would cool down like ice. But the damage, which was done to his spouse repeatedly by denigrating her self-respect and status in front of the entire household including the servants and maids, was something irreparable. You, therefore, always taught us, "A done deed, a thrown arrow and a spoken word can never come back." You also often quoted, "World is an echo, so give to the world the best you can."

Ramakrishna Paramhansan once said that s(he) who forbears lives, and s(he) who does not, gets ruined. You kept up utmost faith in these lines. Whenever we provoked you to raise your voice against injustice, you coolly cited these lines. But mother, I have now started doubting the authenticity of these lines. How long can one tolerate? Secondly, what is the guarantee that after long years of forbearance, God will one day come to save you from the ruins and punish the exploiter? Even if God would turn up one day, in a finite space does not it mean the eleventh hour for the individual? And at that point even God would be helpless to undo the wrongs that have been caused to someone. He himself is also bound by the laws he has created for everyone — what has already been damaged cannot be revived at least when you consider the finite span of human life. And there is no need to interpret things with an infinite horizon because in the long run we are all dead. There is no end to rationalisation — one can keep arguing, God would set one free from all exploitation caused to the individual all through his life so that suffering won't be able to touch his mind. But that sort of an argument never fascinates me. I believe in, 'live and let others live'. If someone torments me, I would try to work out its solution, rather than leaving it to the mercy of God. If there is any God, let him remain in peace, let not my action be put to sleep, holding God's future action as a substitute for my present action. But our action has severe limitations. Even if one knows he is cent per cent correct, circumstances can still go entirely against him. Yes, in such a situation prayers do help to uphold the victory of truth over falsehood. We cannot, therefore, afford to depend entirely on our action, as we cannot leave everything to God. A combination of action, knowledge and devotion is the golden approach, as suggested in *Srimad Bhagabat Gita.*

You rightly said, destructive forces in the universe are much more powerful than what constructive forces can generate. The creation that takes place over millions of years, can be destroyed within a fraction of a second. What honesty cannot get over three decades, dishonesty can serve within a day. What is the incentive to be truthful then? Your answer is, constructive forces are less powerful but they can always stop one from falling into the area where destructive forces manifest themselves in full vigour. Yes, I agree with you completely. The constructive forces are rational, and have protective power and that is why the net outcome is life, not death, though both the forces have been co-existing since time immemorial and would continue to do so forever.

It was the summer of 1980. I had just finished my morning tea and was gazing at the news paper, when I found our grand mother Sudha removing all our study materials from the cupboard very confidently. I was shocked, "Who gave her the right to throw away all our books without even asking us once about their usefulness?" Didi pounced on her as soon as she saw her Shakespeare lying in the dust and getting ready to be sold off to the garbage-picker. But she retaliated with double of her normal strength and vigour insisting that more space is required for keeping useful things in the cupboard. What was most surprising was that all other family members joined Sudha. Raji's support was obviously understandable. But how could others do this? Seeing Didi's anger father started scolding her; in fact as it went he supported grandma altogether. Father's point initially was that Didi must not speak in that manner. But what do you do when no one is ready to listen to your viewpoint? Sometimes rudeness is required to protect one's right. But rationality had disappeared. Everyone, except you, was supportive of Sudha. I gave it up; if this is the level of conscience of the elders, truth can never prevail in this family. I spoke to myself and decided to keep quiet.

Two days later suddenly grandma started screaming early in the morning that because of us resources are getting wasted like anything. I could not make out the head or tail of the issue. I did not know what the context was. Much later, after several months, I had discovered that all this was pre-planned by Raji. Grandma would unnecessarily pick up faults with us, for no reason, and start shouting when we would retaliate to justify the truth. The entire household would see how rude and rough we were. How wayward we had become. And all this was due to your instigation. You were to be held responsible for spoiling us and polluting our mind against the elders in the family. Father would get convinced by this and hence, he would soon command us not to be in your company. Thus, you would be left altogether alone in the ocean of danger and jealousy.

Their plan succeeded partly. Father's behaviour followed their grand design. He almost uttered the same vowels that Raji used to put into grandma's mouth, "Children have been spoilt and absolutely wayward because of the mother." Thus, Raji had succeeded in building a strong case against you on the basis of which you could be thrown out of the house. If not thrown out, the lack of company of your husband and children would put you to mental illness and would also help your in-laws enhance their physical torture on you. Both the goals would be attained with one stroke. What else does one need? Goal would be attained without any damage to the goal-setter's reputation — or to put it differently, others' goal would be attained through your own deeds, rather misdeeds as they all would appear to the world!

Almost a week had passed. Father did not speak to us at all. You kept gazing through the window at the sky, at the trees. Didi thought of visiting some of her friends. She asked you for some money in order to pay for the rickshaw fare; you looked into your purse — there was not a single pie. She still decided to go and see Kanta, thinking that she would take a small loan from her. When she returned home it was early evening. As soon as she entered the premises, father shouted at her. Sudha added, "Girls who study English are often obstinate and disrespectful. It is all mother's instigation." She shouted back, "Don't I have the right to visit my friends. It was only a matter of two hours, and Kanta's house is not in the other end of the world; it is only one-fourth kilometre from our home." Father would not withstand back answering. He readily announced that she must leave the house at once. She also lost her head. She turned back and put on her sandals. Raji's joy knew no bound; she was watching everything as a silent-spectator. Quickly she added that characterless girl must not stay at home. I don't know what intuition did strike you. You decided to accompany her and did so without even changing your sari. Raji looked disturbed, she stood in front of you trying to stop you, "Let her go alone you stay back!" You managed to make your way and quickly accompanied Didi. Much later I had realised why Raji was trying to stop you. Had she left the home all alone, it would have been much easier for Raji to spread that she had eloped. Thus, her marriage would have then become an impossible phenomenon. Your company obviously could not allow her to circulate this rumour. On the contrary, when our neighbours saw you two leaving the house and heard screams from the inside chambers, they quickly concluded that both mother and daughter were driven out of the house. Their fingers pointed to Sudha and Raji instantly.

Both of you went to Manjudi's house. She paid the rickshaw-puller and took you two inside. Both Manjudi and her mother gave you a patient hearing. She at once came to the conclusion that our father was under some *tantrik* spell. You looked at her with a strange awe in our eyes : 'What does it mean?' She went on, "uncle is not in his senses. Someone has done something to him. I will take you to a rishi, whom I know; he will confirm it. Wait here, let me prepare some food for both of you. We will talk about it more."

You two came home by 10.00 O'clock. Manjudi led you the way; no one dared to ask anything. It was understood that you were with her. She did not speak to anyone, just wished father insignificantly and left for home as soon as you were upstairs. She met me near the gate and told me everything.

Father did not come to his bedroom that night. When both you and Didi returned we found that one pillow, one blanket and a bed sheet were carried downstairs. Henceforth, father would be sleeping in the living room. Raji was helping the servant to arrange the bed and put the bedstead smoothly. Sudha's enthusiasm knew no bound, after all she had managed to get her son separated from his wife. No, she never wanted that you should be thrown out of the house. Who else would then manage to do the household work. At the same time she wanted that you should not be living like her son's wife. You must look depressed, wear very ordinary clothes, sleep alone, and that would bring Sudha the utmost satisfaction. She could then get all the work done in a commanding tone, not with a request. To put it in a nutshell, you must remain as a maid in the house. Equal status to all leaves no scope for the ruler to rule. Equal status may bring maximisation of family welfare but who cares for that. What is the charm in life unless one can have somebody lying at her feet and begging of her kindness? There is more satisfaction in giving to a beggar of that kind than to a friend. It satisfies her ego whereas pure love to mankind is non-rewarding. This is the motto that Sudha always believed in.

Mother, you watched everything like a statue. Perhaps you were more worried about what Manjudi had said than anything else. “What this *tantrik* spell is? What would be the solution then?” These were some of the questions, which we kept discussing till late night.

I got up before it was dawn. Sudha was screaming that lights were on almost all through the night; who would pay for the electricity bill? We realised that the old lady was keeping a track of our movements. We need to be more careful. Well, we could hardly talk loudly because Raji used to be in the other room in the first floor, next to your bedroom, and her ears were opened even when she sat for meditation.

Manjudi turned up the next day at around 11.00 a.m. You quickly got ready to go out with her to meet the Rishi. When you came back it was already past 2.00 p.m. Sudha had started her record at the high pitch, “People here find this place a hotel, they can enter anytime they want, they can leave anytime they like.” I listened to this non-sense patiently, and dragged you inside the room to hear what the rishi had told you. You untied the knot and showed me some leaves and morning glory flower from the fag end of your sari. The Rishi gave them to you, you said. They need to be folded in a red piece of cloth and placed at the altar. Both in the morning and evening you were supposed to worship in order to invoke the blessings of the Mother Durga. The Rishi refused to tell you anything himself. He suggested that Mother would let us know what exactly the problem was.

The *puja* was performed for twenty-one days as per his instructions and, then one day as I was coming out of your bedroom unmindfully, I found Raji trying to take out threads from your sari, which you had spread outside to dry up. As soon as she saw me she changed her finger movement and pretended that she was trying to make space so that she could also lay her clothes outside. I reported this to you; we decided to go to the Rishi next day with the sari she had already damaged. He examined that portion of the sari from where Raji had detached a small piece, and replied, "So now you know who is the culprit." He urged us to keep faith in Mother — the Mother of the whole universe, who would set every thing right in due course. You wept; with folded hands you said, "Baba my daughter is still unmarried, without my husband's co-operation how can I get her married. My own relatives do not stay here. My son is a kid. I don't have anyone to give us any support." Baba asked you to be patient. He looked at me and advised to take care of you.

Almost six months had passed. Father would hardly look at us. He left my school fees sometimes with Sudha, and sometimes in the rack with a note, "Here is the money," not addressed to any specific individual, only to be understood by the concerned individual.

I could understand the agony you had undergone. What a mental torture! Everyone laughing at you every now and then! Everyone trying to mock you in the pretext of sympathising! I wish, mother, you had a career for yourself. You could have walked out instantly not giving a damn to all this non-sense. This is the fate of millions of women in our country. Several of them are educated but they hardly think of pursuing their career. They try to remain satisfied with the comfort that their husbands have provided. Unfortunately they do not realise that it could be purely transitory. Time in future can be so different from the time at present that repentance would remain as the only outlet. What is the purpose of education if it cannot be used as an asset at the time of your need. And education is such an asset that if it is not cultivated continuously, it ceases to yield. Discontinuity makes the situation as bad as its absence.

Bigger tests were awaiting us, rather you particularly, though in the short run things improved in our favour. Temporary shades are always brighter because colourlessness is something, which is going to emerge subsequently and last forever. One evening, grandma was found shouting at the peak of her voice. Father had requested her to make the payment to the travel agent when he would bring the ticket, but she happened to hand over the money to the wrong person. Perhaps father was unhappy about the incident and Sudha lost her control. Raji joined Sudha, saying "our mother is not here to work as a maid for others in the family. Wife and children are there; they can be asked to deliver these minor services. Why to bother our mother unnecessarily." "Unnecessarily indeed," I thought. My tongue was growing longer to give a befitting reply, "When it comes to money and attention, mother has the monopoly right over them, and when it comes to services then one remembers wife and children! Nothing in the world is free of cost. You want everything. You have to give something at least in return." You pulled me inside the room, and placed your hands on my mouth. "Please don't say anything, we have bad times, it is all our destiny. Keep quiet. God will answer our prayers one day," you said.

Perhaps God answered our prayers, temporarily though. Father gradually became normal day by day and started sharing his time with us and a time came, when he almost didn't look at Raji. To Sudha it was only his duty that he had to do as a son.

One evening when we were all spending time together in the terrace, father whispered that Raji, Prabhat and Sudha had planned a big game against us. Quickly you intervened "what is it? Again, some new problem?" Father said, "Last night when I was about to sleep in the living room, I heard Prabhat suggesting them to claim that the ornaments kept in the family locker belonged to them : all those are their property. We can't do anything because there is no legal proof that the gold belongs to us." Mother, you almost burst into tears, "My daughter is not married yet. This is all that I have for my daughter. How can I part with it? My father gave this to me at the time of my marriage, not for my in-laws but for myself and my family." Father tried to console you, "Don't worry, no one can snatch away our fate. They can only take away our money and gold, which we can always acquire, if we are destined to." You wept, "No, I can't get over the shock of losing my ornaments given by my parents during the time of my marriage." I suggested that you talk to uncle Arun but as we learnt later, it was to be of no use. Uncle Arun was playing the role of Bhisma and Drona in *Mahabharata*. Knowing fully well what is right and wrong, he decided to keep quiet and, unwillingly though, he respected his mother's ideas. Or to put it differently he was not willing to go against his mother, sister and uncle. Father was quite disheartened to learn this. But there was no alternative before us. What cannot be cured must be endured.

Their main objective was to secure the future of Sudha and Raji, and Prabhat's suggestion was to assure it by grabbing. But there was another side of the story, which was to torture father and you. They knew that both of you would be quite shaken by this attempt of theirs. You might lose your mental balance also. The amount was not negligible, and hence your tears would bring them great joy. Grandma thought father would have to buy gold from the market for Didi's marriage and thus he would exhaust himself once he would get her married. Both of you would then stay in Cuttack house for ever serving them religiously and faithfully without even being able to think of buying or constructing another house anywhere else.

Raji had a different idea. If Didi's marriage could be postponed forever, then she could also serve them all through her life. When you would become old, she would then start taking the responsibility of the kitchen. Eventually she must take your role in the family. But for that to happen she must not go for higher studies and pursue her career. She must lose her reputation so that she would not remain any more eligible in the marriage market.

One day you discovered a bunch of hair, nail and some other dirty stuff lying below Didi's pillow on the bed. When you asked the Rishi, he confirmed that all that was done to make her mind disturbed. Neither should she be able to concentrate on her studies nor should she be able to observe self-control. And that would serve Raji's purpose very well. God alone knows what would have happened ultimately had they remained there for long. I can say only this much that when the stuff was removed from her bed she continued to sleep peacefully. I am sure Raji must have felt quite frustrated to note this.

She focussed all her energies to spread rumours about Didi. One day, when I returned from the college I found you crying. When I asked you the reason repeatedly, you mentioned that you heard Raji telling our neighbour atrocious things against Didi. The main content was that she had become pregnant, and father had to take her to the hospital for an abortion. I asked you to just ignore all this non-sense, and not to convey to father anything of that sort. I knew father would be more disheartened to know the enmity and jealousy of his nearer ones. Besides, the whole purpose of his idea of discipline would be ruined, and no one can witness the death of his faith that he has believed in all through his life. Howsoever, ridiculous it might have been, father was extraordinarily strict with us mainly because of his deep concern for us : no one should be able to say a single nasty word about us. If he would learn that this was what Raji was spreading he would lose his sanity. He might not hesitate to literally throw her out of the balcony. In order to seek peace for the household and its members I requested you to drink this poison by yourself. Didi was not affected because untrue things, howsoever, dangerous they are, could not bother her at all. Perhaps, I was too young to understand the outcomes of those rumours and especially their intensity. Adversity unknown or not understood is indeed a blessing in disguise. After several months of her marriage this was disclosed to father; till then you kept the poison in your throat my darling mother!

It was not that father was totally unaware of the rumours that Raji was trying to implant in people's mind. Cuttack is a small city, after all they had reached him in some form or the other if not as crudely as you had heard. But keeping in view Didi's sentiments he had decided not to disclose to us. At least this much he was aware of that Raji was trying to break all her marriage proposals. Once, do you remember, father asked Didi to come and meet one elderly person in his chamber? She followed you and spend a few minutes there. After she came back, while both you and father were still chatting with the gentleman, I could see from the window of the room in the first floor that Raji was standing behind the curtain and was focussing on your conversation. After spending a few minutes there she went out. Probably she was trying to identify who the person was, what could be his possible mailing address so that she could send him a couple of letters enlightening him about

Didi's character which Raji had created in her imagination. Also, she wanted to know the name of the gentleman because her *tantrik* would need it in any case to cast spell and break the negotiation.

After almost a month of Didi's marriage, Sudha was talking to Phuti in her living room, and I happened to be outside the room, just in front of the window. I heard her saying, "Raji tried so hard to stop the marriage but could she? It is actually a 'yog', marriage is a 'samyog', once the `yog' comes, no one can stop it." I had told you this, "if they have so much knowledge then why try to cause harm to others? Unfortunate lots"!

But such characters are those who spend days after days in the place of worship. Raji would go and stay in the Ramakrishna Math, Bhubaneshwar, weeks after weeks. Initially I used to think that this strife she was pursuing for self-improvement. But later I reasoned out the actual cause. If she would spend most of her time in religious activities no one should ever suspect her that she could do such heinous activities. Everyone would think, 'how pious she is'! Some may know that she is quarrelsome but no one should have even an ounce of doubt that she could step down to this level. Besides, those who invoke the evil power to cause harm to others they have the fear that the destructive force may retaliate on them. So they seek shelter in holy places. After all what this destructive science is? It is an art, which the ancient Indians had mastered, and it has existed since then. The Atharva Vedas comprise this mysterious form of knowledge. It invokes the unsatisfied spirits to fulfill certain objectives of the invoker. Yes, God is there but he is miles away from us. The spirits are relatively closer to us. Unless one is exceptionally devotional, the *tantrik* spell can affect the individual to some extent if not entirely. Besides,

God is indifferent to individuals' actions and reactions, as stated in the *Gita*. Neither he performs any action on any one's behalf nor does he suggest one to pursue any specific activity. However, for his true devotees he can do whatever is required. But we are ordinary human beings. Where can we find so much love for God? As Tagore said, "To keep You in my heart where will I find that enormous amount of love, my lord!" Yes, we may only keep trying to seek His love and concern. As I mentioned this to you, you sobbed profoundly, I remember.

After a couple of years when she understood that we were partly aware of her misdeeds, she, in order to weaken your faith in God, would speak in your hearing range, "The great man like Swamiji (Vivekananda) was also affected by the *tantrik* spell, cast on him by the Fakir in Kashmir. What about ordinary human beings then? He had to leave Kashmir at once as soon as he started vomiting blood. He asked the Holy Mother Sarada Devi with a deep emotional outburst that Thakur did not protect him. The Holy Mother replied that it was an art, and Thakur respected all forms of art and religion in the world. So, he could not have made it ineffective."

Raji's point was clear. Whatever spiritualism you may practice, the impact of *tantrik* spell that she would cast should bear adverse repercussions on you. The entire *tantrik* spell actually works through the psychological process, and she was trying desperately to affect your nervous system. Once you would be weak, and start losing faith in God, you would be in her clutches. But I admire your love for God. Even when things went entirely against us, you held him right close to your heart. As a result Raji remained unsuccessful for several years in driving you insane and making you bed-ridden. Her focus then changed from you to father. The only way to punish you was to cause harm to father. If he would fall sick or face even worse adversities, then your morale would be shattered. But in the process, she did not realise that she was ruining her own brother. Who cares? Evil mind knows no relationship. The goal had to be attained by any means. But what was surprising was Prabhat's continuous misguidance and miscreants without an ounce of repentance and Sudha's strong support to Raji. How could a mother think of bringing devastation to her worthy son? Scriptures say, son can be a black ship but a mother is always a divine angel for her son. I think these are just for 'loksikhsya'. Mothers can also be dangerous, otherwise so many daughters-in-law in our society would not have been dying of burns. Yes, in several occasions the son is also a party to it but in many other instances mothers do it all by themselves. Does the mother think then that in the process she is ruining her son's life? Yes, she may find a new bride with much more dowry for her son but what about the agony of the son he undergoes when he loses his wife. Well, in our society men are not supposed to be emotional fools. They should be pragmatic. So, whatever the mother does, it is justified. Several daughters-in-law live in perpetual unhappiness. Sometimes they are driven out of the home and are compelled to stay away from their husbands in the rest of their life. Not always husbands appreciate this. But they have no voice because then the mothers remind them of their duties and the care that the mothers had shown when the sons were infants. Men at times have been forced to endorse their mothers' views on their wives, and decisions too. Whatever scriptures may say, sometimes women in our society proved to be the worst enemies of their children. Our grandma is one of the brightest examples of this.

Raji started slow poisoning father. After you would come out of the kitchen, Sudha would first go behind the kitchen to make sure that no one was around. Then she would give some indication, which Raji could only understand. She used to take something in a bottle, hiding it under her *sari*. She would pour it into the container in which the curry was served for father. As father returned from the hospital late in the afternoon, his food used to be kept separately as soon as the cooking was over so that it remained at least warm till he had his lunch. Therefore, Raji never faced any inconvenience to add the mixture into father's food. She was always clever to add it to the best dish of the day so that father would not miss it by any chance. Mother, we were too foolish to understand the game. When we learn from the cook, who had seen it accidentally in a couple of occasions, it was too late. The cook himself also had not understood it thoroughly. Only after seeing the consequences he was convinced of what he had hypothesised, and then disclosed to us.

Within a few months father started looking quite dull. I asked you several times whenever you both came to see me in Delhi, "Ma, why does he look so lifeless?" You could hardly answer. At the most you would say, "Perhaps because of tension." "What tension?," I would retort back, "Now that Didi is married and settled, and I am here in Delhi for my higher studies father should be feeling free."

Ma, Raji is, indeed, a crooked female. She didn't give you the poison because in that case father could have had an investigation made on your health and identified the actual cause. But when the doctor himself is sick there is none to treat him. Whenever I asked him about his poor health, he attributed it to the age factor. People don't look so old in early fifties, and secondly, how could it happen within a few months? After Didi's marriage and my departure from Cuttack Raji had a gala time to implement all her ideas. I should have suspected some evil plan, and should have cautioned you accordingly. How could I forget what she was trying to do on Didi's marriage day. She was about to add some intoxicants in the 'kheer' that was prepared for her when Kum Kum, her friend, saw it and cautioned her. As she would have consumed it, she would have lost her senses. The groom finding her ill and senile would have gone back from the marriage altar itself. What a shame would it have been on father! Then he must have had a heart attack and lied on the bed. This would have been the right lesson for you, as Raji thought. But God did not approve of her plan. He listened to your prayers at least in the short-run. Besides, how can I forget those ashes and charcoal that Raji was trying to associate with Didi's *benarsi,* that she was supposed to wear for her wedding. Again, Gopa pisi saw it and cautioned me. I ran to the Rishi with her saree. He had said that the ashes were collected from the burning ghat by a *tantrik* and Raji planned a severe set back with his help. Anyway the Rishi poured holy water from Goddess's *kalash* on her saree, and she wore it finally. When I was knowing all this, it should have struck me right away that father's illness was caused my some unnatural process. Father himself also could not make out what his illness was? Otherwise I am sure he would have had a proper check-up. You also did not take the matter seriously else you would have asked the Rishi for a remedy. After all you yourself were suffering in that furnace. It was difficult for you to assess everything minutely.

You thought father needed a change desperately. Once he would go out, he would be alright. You wanted him to look for a job in Delhi so that we all could stay together as Didi's husband was also supposed to get a transfer to Delhi. Father became desperate to leave Cuttack but before moving to Delhi, he thought of completing the construction of a small house in

Bhubaneshwar. He always maintained that in future some of us might require a place to stay. And as the situation was developing, the Cuttack house, he thought, would become increasingly inaccessible to us even to spend a few days. He was right in this respect; father had a tremendous foresight though he did not act accordingly in certain occasions thus paying a heavy toll through his own life, and his wife and children's life too.

Phuti had emerged as a major power by then. Her sons were settled, her period of struggle was over. She raised the frequency of her visits to our house extending her moral support to Raji, Sudha and Prabhat. She always wanted that only her family should rise, her sons should emerge in the society as the brightest stars, the rest should go to hell. When it came to others, her every sentence began with a disgusting expression, "Oh so and so, his/her son is a rouge, a goon, a road side romeo, a 'laphanga', a street urchin...." It is good to be the well-wisher of one's own children but what good does it serve by degrading others? Yes, that is the philosophy of the fools. By degrading others they feel much superior to the rest.

She found golden opportunity to vent out the frustrations of her life. She could never stand you wearing colourful clothes and travelling with father in his car since she was deprived of all these pleasures. You, however, took a liking for her and cared for her with great compassion and sympathy. But the great oak tree of greed was spreading its branches in her mind. She thought if father could be eliminated from the house, she could then ask for a lion's share in the family property. As long as father would be alive, she would not have a face to ask for it explicitly.

She almost stopped talking to you whenever she came to join the post-lunch sessions with her mother and sister. On the contrary, she started instigating Raji more and more against you and us. She recollected old episodes to highlight your follies and cooked up vulgar comments on Raji allegedly made by you. Father's aunt told me these things much later. You, perhaps, still continue to see Phuti with an eye of kindness. But God alone knows how unscrupulous and cruel she had been. For no solid reason she wanted to see you ruining. After paying several visits to Ramakrishna Math and after Father's aunt's sweet advice Raji at times did cool down and tried to overcome the poison she had in her mind. But Phuti ignited her continuously. She was waiting eagerly like a vulture to eat the corpses of family property. Raji's property, she knew, she would inherit if she could extend all her support to her. On the contrary, she kept saying nasty things against Raji to us polluting our mind and biasing us constantly against her. In the fight of two, the third party would be the gainer : she understood it better than anyone else on the earth. Besides, she knew that Raji had access to the powerful *tantrik*. If some of the good things of our life can be transferred to her sons and their suffering can be transferred to us through *tantrik* spell, it would bring her immense pleasure. She had heard from her in-laws that such things were possible, thus, believed in them strongly.

She pastured Raji, by all means. She prepared 'dahibara', 'pistaka' and 'aludam' for Raji and fed her with all sincerity. She had learnt that her elder son was destined to meet with an accident, which could prove to be fatal. So, her desperation was to transfer that misfortune to some of our lives and make his son lead a comfortable life. This is the tragedy of Indian civilisation. We started with an attitude of universal love. Our ancient *slokas* read :

सर्वेभवन्तु सुखिनः, सर्वे सन्तु निरामयाः।
सर्वे भद्राणि पश्यन्तु, मा कश्चिद् दुःखभाग्भवेत्।।
"*sarve bhavantu sukhina*
sarve santu niramaya
sarve bhadrani pasyantu
ma kashid dukha bhag bhavet."

But we seem to be ending that era with a strong selfish motive. It is even worse than that because by being selfish one does not wish ill to others; one is only concerned with one's own welfare. But here one is trying for his/her welfare by casting evil on others. We often criticise the Westerners saying that theirs is an individualistic society, and ours is based on the spirit of universal brotherhood. We even extend our love to animals, plants and all living beings :

वनस्पतयः शान्तिर्विश्वेदेवाः शान्तिर्ब्रह्म शान्तिः।
"*Banaspataya shanti*
Biswe devaa shanti"

But there is a huge gap between what we preached once and what we practice today. At least the Westerners are honest enough to reveal their objective of maximisation of individual utility. Hypocrisy is the worst possible disease of mankind and when it grows rapidly, the end is almost certain. That is why I say we are ending our civilisation with something that was inconceivable by our sages.

Apart from her greed for property there was also something in Phuti's mind, which I find difficult to express. It is not exactly similar to Raji's feelings. In case of Raji it was causeless malignancy, her inability to withstand others prosperity and progress. On the other hand, for Phuti, it was a kind of satisfaction that women derive by causing harassments or suffering to other women. Particularly, those who are deprived of certain happiness in life tend to develop this attitude towards their in-laws especially. Of course, not all are of this kind. There are women who become extra affectionate towards others thinking that what they could not get in life, others must attain it. And if they could help others attain such happiness in life, it would be their greatest satisfaction. But unfortunately your in-laws were not like that. Phuti's sweet behaviour could never generate any doubt in the mind of the outsiders. Always she looked concerned but passed a sigh of relief as soon as she heard something bad had happened to some one in her circle. Her mind always awaited such news eagerly. Whenever I told you about her characteristics you avoided the topic. You held strongly that it is a sin to judge others in terms of a standard scale of measurement : particularly when one could not lead a normal life, we must try to understand her viewpoint as well. It is sometimes very propelling for such people to take the world as the cause of their suffering : their subconscious mind draws a kind of solace by seeing others suffering.

But as one grows up, shouldn't one learn to overcome these problems of the mind? We have the capabilities to control our thoughts, and that is why we are human beings. Phuti never made any conscious effort to improve her mind. Even when she witnessed the brighter days of her life, her attitude grew worse. Imagine, such a state of mind with arrogance! Actually goodness or badness does not have much to do with happiness or misery : it all matters on the mental strength. Even Heavens cannot bestow peace on someone who is fundamentally wrong. Look at Raji, even after visiting Ramakrishna Math so frequently, spending months in the company of sages and intellectuals and, more importantly even after getting the special opportunities to remain close to the sanctum sanctorum, the state of mind did not change. On the contrary, she interpreted things in more ridiculous ways : such opportunities to participate in spiritual discourses and sometimes even to deliver lectures on Sri Ramakrishna gave her a feeling that God has a special love for her, hence, what she was doing was not actually unjustified or fundamentally wrong. Otherwise such opportunities would not have dropped in her hands. Besides, she thought that Arjun also had to kill his relatives, and Krishna actually asked him to do so. So why could not she? This is what she learnt after reading Gita. Unfortunate soul, she failed to recognise the cause of action, which actually determines its rightness and wrongness. I tell you Ma, too much of scriptures and spiritual text for half educated characters and ignorant souls are dangerous than the nuclear bombs of destruction — they actually denigrate them rather than serving any good. Besides, the individuals associated with them too are affected miserably. Meanness with an excess of religiosity can be more dangerous than a black cobra.

Phuti was annoyed with the rest of the world because she was alleged to be involved in an affair with her brother-in-law. Yes, I can see a point in her reaction. After all a widow at a young age she was. On the other hand, her brother-in-law was a bachelor staying under the same roof. The world did not try to understand their situation while forming criticisms. But the main issue is even when her husband was alive, she had developed an affair with her brother-in-law. And this started right after her marriage when her husband was away for a few weeks. Such a divinc and thorough gentleman her husband was; unfortunately he did not find Phuti trustworthy. What a shock it must have been to him. Phuti's mother-in-law, as soon as she could substantiate her suspicion with evidence, called for her son and sent her off. Of course, Phuti's brother-in-law is also to be blamed equally, and from that point of view I do not think the criticism of the society was impartial though both were often the hot topics in the gossiping circles. What I could never approve was her flirtatious nature, which allowed herself to romance with her brother-in-law while the husband was perfectly alright. Bubbles of passion can arise in the ocean of mind, but one has got to ignore them. After her husband passed away, she continued to have more affairs with her husband's nephews. And as some of her in-laws had disclosed later, the instigation was from her side. I am ready to vouch for her affair with her brother-in-law during the days of her widowhood, but certainly cannot see any reason of flirtation with her husband's nephews, who in terms of status were like her sons. At least that is what the Indian society has taught us for generations. She should have devoted her attention more to her responsibilities to raise her sons than the passion which knew no bound to rush down from the hill-tops of her wayward mind to the pleasure of devastation. Was it not a disgrace to the concept of motherhood? After all what a woman of her kind would understand the concepts of respect and affection? For her, any two individuals of opposite sex if seen together must be romancing. It was quite natural for her to think that two persons moving in the same vehicle were engaged in love-making. May God bless such souls who see the whole world yellow because they themselves suffer from jaundice.

Your second sister-in-law Khuki showed tremendous concern for everyone in the family. She did not belong to any particular camp but unfortunately she could not avoid the impact of Raji on her altogether. Actually, since the grandmother was with Raji, other siblings, directly or indirectly also came in the influence of Raji. At least Khuki's and Arun's position can be explained in this framework. The constant prick given by the mother, and misreporting of all incidents to Arun and Khuki gradually roped them in. Actually a lie said repeatedly by your loved one is as good as truth, and it becomes much stronger in the mind than a fact. Khuki would try to extract all information from us, and would quickly report them to Raji or Sudha. You did not believe me, but I had found her several times playing these tricks against us. Raji had got Khuki as a good information-gathering agent after father's aunt on realising the purpose of Raji's undue curiosity declined to play such a role.

Long back, Khuki asked me one day about the progress of Didi's marriage and innocently I told her the proposals that we had received. She also asked me the details of the proposals and I unravelled them. Soon after she gathered them, she ran to Raji to report. I was in the bathroom and both the sisters were in the storeroom : Raji meticulously took note of the proposals; the conversation is still flashing in my mind. Raji ran to the *tantrik* in the evening to get Didi rejected by all the prospective grooms. Even before my every exam Khuki used to pass on my timetable to Raji, and she would try sincerely to get me flunked in every paper. No, mother, whatever you may say, all the three sisters-in-law of yours contributed generously to cause us damage. When she knew Raji's intention of collecting the information, why didn't she stop it. Those who sin, and those who help them do it are equally guilty. Khuki had no desire for family property but she derived a satisfaction from seeing us suffer. Perhaps, she was frightened by the fact that Raji would not let her stay in peace if she did not co-operate with her. In exchange of her personal comfort perhaps she entered into an implicit bargain with Raji. But even after realising that Raji did not spare her either, when it came to material prosperity, she did not give up her habit. You mean to say that Khuki didn't know how Raji made all possible attempts ranging from *tantrik* means to biological factors, to rule out the possibilities of her conception? Sudha herself told me once, "Khuki is too old to conceive now. She does not realise this; she is growing unusually obstinate. Does she have the mental strength and stamina to rear a child. She has the desire but does not have the patience to withstand the pain." Can a mother say such a thing about her own daughter to others? The main reason was that if Khuki would have cherished motherhood, then she would not have stayed in Orissa at all. Her husband must have forced her to give up the job and settle in Assam. The very thought of this possibility made Raji and Sudha both brood over their future. Who would look after them in case they fall sick? Yes, that insecurity feeling is there in every human being, particularly in the old age, but does it justify planning ill for others.

Mother, I am aware of the fact that both Sudha and Raji influenced Nabu not to take Khuki to the specialist he knew in Calcutta. Well, when father took her to the gynecologist, they could not say directly anything to him but lectures on self-control, spiritualism and philosophy did gain momentum within the household. Anyway, the tragedy is that even after experiencing all this, Khuki did not leave their company. I must say that Sudha had very obedient daughters who supported her even when she was grossly wrong.

Do you mean to say Khuki was not aware of slow poisoning of father, planned by Raji? May be yes : I would agree with you on that front. Raji did not take anyone into confidence except Sudha in such matter. But Prabhat must have been aware of each and every development at our place. In fact, without his support Raji could not have mastered up so much courage to implement her scheme.

Sometimes, I used to think that I must follow Raji to the *tantrik* she visited, and would ask him "Why do you try your art on us? If you have so much power why can't you utilise it for curative or constructive purposes? What is the big deal in bringing damage to others?" But that is the tragedy : this art is primarily destructive. No, it would be wrong to suggest so; actually people who usually practise and acquire this power are the dropouts of the school of spirituality. In the path of a practising spiritualist these powers, as Ramakrishna mentions, would come automatically but a true spiritualist is not expected to devote his attention to these petty achievements. S(he) must ignore them and aspire for what he called *suddha bhakti* (pure and unconditional devotion), which can help attain and retain God in the heart of the seeker. Unfortunately many of the travellers in this path decide to give up after climbing a few steps, which help them acquire such power. This power can be utilised for both good and bad purposes but since most of the dropouts are basically not high quality minded individuals, they utilise their power for destructive purposes only. Besides, it is the human tendency to see the outcomes of an action immediately. Incidentally, resources/energies utilised for constructive purposes start yielding only after a long gestation period whereas destruction is instantaneous; it takes no time to witness its outcomes. Both the practitioners and the customers of this art are aware of this, and so they use it extensively to settle scores with their enemies. No law can punish them, none can even have the slightest doubt, only the adverse effects will be felt on the individuals that they dislike.

Very clearly the Rishi had advised you, I recall, that we must not even think of visiting such *tantrik* for solutions to our problems. The reply for an adverse action must not be in similar terms. Patience and tolerance are the strongest shields that protect us from adversities. Ramakrishna said that in self-defence we must avoid the wicked ones, but there is no need to cause them any harm. Even in the midst of suffering if we could pray sincerely to God, the Rishi we had visited said, we can invoke the blessings of the almighty and no *tantrik* spell can harm us in that case. Gurudeva's (Swami Vireswarananda ji) reply to my letter in this respect brought me enormous solace : "Sri Sri Thakur has taken you in His benign protection, no *tantrik* spell can harm you in the least."

Even several years after the hurdle I faced first in my life in communicating my ideas/views to others, I continued to have similar problems. I would either keep quiet in the middle of a conversation or choose to be a silent and patient listener. It was not that I didn't understand the depth of the conversation, rather it was so that I could not recollect words at that particular moment which could display my thoughts skilfully. Very many lucrative opportunities had come up in my life but because of the constraint of language I had to step back. I know you had struggled a lot to provide us with better quality education. Having been raised in a state, that speaks a language other than your mother tongue, you had realised how important English is for exchanging our views among Indians, not to talk of people from other countries. I remember, how you wept days after days and continued your hunger strike until father agreed to reconsider the issue of changing our schools. The influence of grandmother and Raji on father was enormous. Their argument was, those who go to English medium schools, emerge as arrogant crooks and later on they are the ones who bring disgrace to the family. On the other hand, your vision was wide. You wanted your children to move out from the narrow boundaries of caste, colour, creed, clime and religion and region; you wanted them to travel across the globe; you wanted them to learn from the rest of the world and speak to the rest of the world the great cultural heritage India possesses. However, people were not ready to understand your viewpoint; even if they did, they did not endorse it. You decided to settle the matter with your partial success on the issue — some of us were shifted to a school where the medium of instruction was vernacular, and some were fortunate enough to continue in the English medium schools.

Prabhat's children went to some third rate schools, for they were not interested in studies. And he could not withstand the fact that we all could be sent to good schools — holding bright careers and future prospects. Raji could not stand that some of us someday in future may hold a job better than hers. Grandmother thought about the expenses that an English medium school would cost *vis-a-vis* a municipal school and made serious calculations on amounts that she could save from father's income and allocate the funds towards the welfare of her other children. And we became the ultimate resting place of the spill over of all this meanness.

Whenever I complained to you about the problems I faced in expressing my ideas you kept helping me as much as you could. Raji would mock at us; grandmother would burn us alive if looks could do so. I can understand the latter's psychology : at the back of her mind she knew pretty well that she was illiterate and what illiteracy meant; at the core of her heart she understood the differences between those who are literate and those illiterate; at the inner most part of her soul she felt depressed, "I wish, I were also literate and educated!" She must have cursed her parents, the society she was raised, and the circumstances that might have happened to be the immediate cause of her suppression. Her expressions were nothing but the revolution against something she perhaps hated the most but endorsed because she had no choice. She was made to believe in something, which she would have perhaps discarded right in the beginning of her youth if alternatives/ options were available to her. Her hatred towards education is natural — an outcome of a complex situation that continuously tormented her inner self. She challenged the masculine order in the depth of her intellect, while expressing anger towards persons of same sex.

But Raji's feelings cannot be rationalised in the same framework. She is an epitome of cruelty, meanness and jealousy of the human mind which would cut across gender, race and intellect, which remains subtle in some form or the other beneath the satin globes of our aristocracy that we acquire to cleverly hide our deformities of the mind, which requires constant struggle with the self to be won over, which alone by the practice of self-analysis can be reduced to minimum tolerable heights. In addition, she represents that component of weakness of the human mind, which allows itself to be exploited by the opposite sex in exchange of the support it desires to draw for its manifestation on the destructive plane. A constant vigilance on the self and efforts to generate constructive ideas can only outweigh the destructive quality of the human mind, and make us different from what can be described as brutal instincts usually symbolised by furious animals. Prabhat is the male counterpart of what Raji represents among women. However, the difference between the two can be explained in terms of frustration overwhelmingly present in Prabhat, and in terms of vindictiveness, predominantly present in Raji.

Raji's main grievance against you was that you were the first person to have noticed her misconduct. If you have not noticed anything, her revengeful attitude would perhaps have been slightly less intense towards you. The fact that she knew that you had noticed her weaknesses, helped her imagine a degradation of her image in the eyes of other relatives. Your quietness over the issue did make her realise that you did not attach much importance to the issue, but she could not get over the fact that it was already recorded in your mind. At least in front of you she thought, it would not be possible for her any more to raise her image to the status of a prophet.

It was a Sunday morning — raining heavily since previous night. The maid, Malamma had not come to work. The worry was, who would do the cleaning? None in the household was as worried as grandma, though the female folk except Raji looked slightly upset. You came down from your bedroom and decided to get into the job. Raji, perhaps felt a little embarrassed and quickly exclaimed, "Oh these household work! That's not my cup of tea. Anyway I have not got into 'samsara', I don't have to bother about all this." Grandma was in a good mood, she was perhaps pleased to note that you had released her worry. She quickly retorted, "Well God has given you a stomach. Irrespective of whether you have a 'samsara' or not, you need to carry out certain basic activities as long as the body exists." Raji twisted her mouth in disapproval — more than disapproval was her anger on the fact that her mother supported someone who did not deserve it. Too many words of praises for the daughter-in-law invoked by the mother-in-law would certainly spoil the former.

A day later Malamma turned up. Grandma's queries poured in. With great difficulty and hesitation Malamma replied that it was her father-in-law who expressed his brutal desire to sleep with her, and that led to a major conflict in the family. On hearing her story everyone in our family burst into laughter. Grandmother made a couple of sarcastic comments on

Malamma's father-in-law but no one expressed any real concern for her. More than anyone else you were embarrassed to hear her story. Her husband was in the bed for last four months as he had met with an accident and had a major fracture in his knee. The poor lady was running the household, which perhaps was becoming increasingly difficult for her. You could soon realise that it was her dependence on father-in-law's income, which prompted him with great intensity to stretch his desire too far. Raji opposed you and asked you to shut up, as there was no need, according to her, to intervene into the maid's private life. You held your position tight. The fact that someone is being tortured and exploited unduly outraged you, and all your support you extended to the poor lady. Very soon other male members of the household realised their responsibilities, and our father urged uncle to speak to Malamma's father-in-law directly. Soon he was sent for, and uncle Arun warned him that he might be handed over to the police if a single complain he would get to hear about his misconduct. Things changed overnight and Malamma greeted you with respect. You also requested father to look into her financial problems. I am sure, if you had the resources you would have emptied all your treasure to save the poor lady. But you too were helpless. Good thoughts can translate themselves into good action only when resources are available. Anyway a heart without resources is more useful for the society than resources without heart.

Resources without heart are often unproductive and destructive. If they are not manned properly they can ruin life in no time. Raji had energies as well as the financial strength but she lacked a constructive mind. In stimulating her destructive attitude Prabhat's role needs to be undermined. He constantly brain washed her against the rest of the family members, particularly against father and us. Prabhat used the most dangerous weapon that is, the fear of becoming homeless in the old age. His constant preaching against us made Raji believe strongly that once grandfather would pass away, the entire property would be grabbed by our father and we would in no time throw her out of the house. A single lady without shelter in her old age would then have to face the whole world all by herself! The fear grabbed Raji, she refuted vehemently though. She emphatically argued that God would stand by her in the bad times. But unknowingly she had become the victim of the fear that Prabhat had implanted in her mind and nurtured it whenever an opportunity rose. Prabhat had a master plan : if Raji would remain in his clutches, he, rather his son, would be able to grab Raji's possessions. The best policy for this was to frighten her and then dictate the terms in the garb of a well-wisher. But Raji could not understand the motive of Prabhat. Her jealousy perhaps did not allow her to take a rational stand and understand the complexities of the problem. Seeing father's progress particularly after his return from Vellore, Raji became increasingly uncontrollable within her heart as she witnessed your material prosperity. Her airtight mind accepted all the filth that Prabhat had to offer and preserved them afresh to cause damage to you in particular. In ruining you if she were to destroy her brother or nephew or anyone for that matter she did not care. Both Prabhat and Raji became complementary to each other; the difference was while Prabhat understood Raji's mind through and through, Raji took Prabhat as her greatest well-wisher on earth. Prabhat promised her the old-age care and support and provided her with avenues to manifest her ideas.

The scriptures were interpreted according to convenience. And the best way to rope in someone in a Hindu orthodox family is to quote from scriptures and attach an unduly long appendix of explanation for listeners to fall victims of their own weaknesses, enabling them to feel the justification of their wishes which otherwise one would have tried to discard them right at the time of their conception. Grandmother was gradually pulled into the pandemonium, making her aware of the possibilities of becoming penniless in future. The implicit property right she had enjoyed all through her life, the status of the household-head, *Kartri* or *Ginni*, that she acquired soon after the death of her mother-in-law and the retirement of grandfather — both coinciding with each other almost perfectly — and the participation of most of her children in the job market, would be washed away, and you would rule the house! She witnessed darkness in the broad daylight! She felt she would be saved if Raji could inherit her position rather than you. But you were the eldest daughter-in-law! How could you be bypassed? "Yes, there is a way," both Prabhat and Raji suggested. If most of the family members including father could be convinced that you were insane, the rest of the events would follow automatically. In addition, if we could emerge as spoilt brats, father would then have no reason to plan for the future of his family. He would also then join Raji's camp, and we would die the death of social isolation. But more than father their immediate need was to hypnotise uncle Arun. But he was a lawyer, he could easily see through the plying of plans. The best thing, as Prabhat suggested, was, therefore, to convince him that father was trying to grab the property including the agricultural land. Father's service to grandfather was basically guided by a strong motive of expropriation. Though unmarried and mostly inclined to religious institutions with little attachment for material property uncle Arun would then gradually fall prey to the lion's clutches : Prabhat took the entire responsibility of speaking to Arun.

Prabhat's association with Arun dates back to almost thirty years. Uncle-nephew relationship was secondary, more propelling was a friendship between the two. Perhaps the absence of age gap and being a confirmed bachelor Arun maintained a sustained relationship, whereas our father right in his twenties had to deviate from the company of his uncle under the pressure of his studies and career.

Arun tried to dismiss Prabhat's views and suggestions initially. But slow and steady flow can win anything under the sun. While Prabhat played cool in his mission, Raji wanted to see the quick results of her efforts. She thought if disputes between grandmother and us can be ignited frequently, Arun would have no reason to continue his respect for you and affection for us. Also, it would be easier to show father how arrogant and unruly his wife and children had become. After all for an Indian man respect for his mother is the deepest of all. The status of an Indian woman as mother is something that is next to God. Here was the click. Raji got the right catch. She would succeed in her plans. The question was how to set it up, how to raise the conflicts and frequency of differences of opinion that individuals tend to have in a joint family. Since affection is stronger than the differences, a family lasts. If the very foundation of the structure can be weakened, the collapse would follow subsequently.

She continued to work sincerely after thinking about the plan seriously. She took grandmother into confidence and made her believe that you didn't follow the rule of equal distribution of food. Further, you did not take any special care to reduce the volume of wastage (of food materials). On the contrary, you wasted a great deal of cooking oil and stuff like that. You didn't have any sense of measurement. Amount you prepared always varied inversely with taste. As you were wasting the resources of the joint family Raji had every reason to complain.

Grandma who endorsed her views would then start her record from early morning. And your biggest weakness was the equanimity of the morning. Your only luxury in life was to sit in the terrace watching the red ball emerging from the blue horizon. The birds would flock together on the branches of 'champaka' opposite to your terrace. You would then murmur lines from Tagore and Gita before you got ready to begin your household work. But Grandma's shrill voice disturbed your peace of mind and irritated you a great deal. Your patience enabled you to remain indifferent. However, your sub-conscious mind registered the disturbed waves of the unpleasant screams, which kept tormenting you from inside. Gradually your expressions kept changing and the feeling of serenity started disappearing from your face. Your concentration diminished, and you looked pale. Grandma's nagging voice tore you into pieces, "Wicked female, comes from a lowly background, behaves like a Nabab's daughter." Often without taking your name she would keep saying several uncouth words. She pretended as if they were meant for the maid or the women in the neighbourhood.

With the provocation of grandma and Raji, sometimes other members of our household also joined hands in criticising your cooking, your each and every activity — how you combed your hair, how you dried your clothes, how you kept your sandals etc. You ignored them with great tolerance. "Generous neglect," that is the term you repeated always. Whenever we tried to retaliate, you calmed us, "There is much more to look forward to in life." One question, which kept me disturbed always was "Why, why are these people after us? After all what have we done? What is our mistake? We carry out their orders as modestly as we can. We never asked them for any favour. Yet, they are determined to harm us!" I didn't understand that jealousy could be so intense that even without any substantive cause it can try to ruin someone who actually has been rendering service to all within the household. But that is how jealousy is. It requires no justification; it is never based on any substantive reason. It can even be directed to the top most well-wisher mainly because s(he) is generous and holds popularity. Yes, good qualities can be the cause of one's torture in this selfish world. Jesus was made to suffer because he spoke the truth — because he wanted others not to suffer from their ignorance. Perhaps, we were too young at that time to realise the complexities of life. But that is how we were attaining maturity. The nature had implanted her machine, skill-fully designed, within us which was providing us an inward looking approach to life — was enabling us to understand the meaning of life, the simple truth that emerges from the complexities of life. We gradually started becoming indifferent to the nuisance that was happening around us. We developed a thick shield around our mind, which would not allow the daily trifles to affect us. Mother, you perhaps drew some solace from seeing us following your footsteps. You looked relaxed. You would sit with your children on the terrace and enjoy the evening. We would discuss Shelly, Keats, Wordsworth and Tagore. Dusk would set in, darkness would prevail upon us yet we would forget that we had to switch on the lights. So engrossed were we in listening to your lucid elaborations! Quickly Raji would report this to grandma, and she would scream, "Showing off her knowledge — after all we have got an educated daughter-in-law."

Father, realised the tension that was growing all around us. He decided to construct a small house with his savings on the plot he had bought in Bhubaneswar at the time of my birth. You had been suggesting to him to follow it up since long, but he had not paid much serious attention to it. Women pre-empt a crisis much before men do; intuition is stronger in women because physically men are stronger. The inverse relation between the two — many men do not accept it though, but truth is unaffected by whether one believes it or not.

Father discussed the plan with Musha-mistri, and he as an architect offered all possible suggestions that he could. The foundation stone was laid and the news spread like wildfire. Raji decided to stop the work at any cost. Sudha also supported her. But both had two separate reasons with the same goal. Sudha was worried about people's remarks : she was convinced that all relatives and friends would point to the harassment that she had been causing to her son and daughter-in-law, and they would blame her for compelling father to construct a separate house for his family. Raji could not conceive the idea that you would be the head of the new household coming up right in front of her eyes. Oh she would die a hundred death before she could see you in her imagination becoming the central point in the family. She ran to the *tantrik* to stop the construction work in all possible ways. Hurdles after hurdles came up. Sometimes problems were created by the labour, sometimes by the contractor himself and sometimes by the chap who supervised the work. It was not possible for father to travel everyday from Cuttack and supervise the work himself. The chap in charge stole the raw materials as much as he could. Father could not withstand his hand-earned money being wasted like water. He shouted several times at the contractor and others. Sudha's joy knew no bound. Often she commented, "What was the need to construct a house. This is big enough to accommodate everyone. My son, you are unnecessarily getting yourself into trouble and tension." Some other time she commented, "Actually all this was instigated by my daughter-in-law; he has been forced into this unnecessary headache." She also suggested to father one day, "Why don't you sell it off. The plot with the boundary wall and the structure would sell at a high price, and at the same time you would be saved from all these troubles." Father did not pay any attention to her unsolicited advice.

Raji was playing her game very coolly. She did not make any discouraging comment nor did she show any interest in what was going on. But whenever I visited Cuttack, I found her discussing very confidentially with Prabhat about the construction work and updating him about what his *tantrik* had conveyed. Raji made trips to Bhubaneswar to place some bones and other filth in the plot. One day when she was dumping them in a hole, your son-in-law witnessed it. She quickly moved her hands, and said "something got stuck in my sandal; I was just trying to remove it." Your son-in-law later on removed from the hole, the stuff, she had put in. On the other hand, she kept her mission going as far as the adding of poison to father's food was concerned. As you were also running around with father to fasten the construction work, she got ample opportunities to implement her scheme.

Sudha kept using adjectives addressing you generously. 'Gharbhangi' (the one who breaks the home) was the most popular one. You never felt like responding to what she said. With all your strength and sincerity you kept helping father, on the one hand, and praying to God on the other. In spite of several major hurdles, which proved almost impossible to be crossed, the construction work ended in the month of September/ October 1985. A single storey house with three bedrooms and a living room with a beautiful lawn outside, was completed. Father passed a sigh of relief. You looked cheerful.

You suggested to father to take his mother and aunt one day and show them the new house. Ma, you didn't realise that that was the beginning of your Doom's day. Father's aunt, was full of praise, she liked the house very much and blessed you immensely. Sudha was also quite impressed by the planning of the house. She immediately started comparing the Cuttack house with the new one, and uttered repeatedly that Father's house had a large number of merits. In the process she started scolding her father-in-law who had initiated the construction of the main building in Cuttack. "Old man had no sense. Didn't he realise that the *verandah* needs to be covered — in the rains how much we suffer!" I quickly corrected her that our great grandfather was never an old-man. He died young at the age of 42, when our grandfather was only 10 years old. Sudha did not pay any attention to what I said. She kept comparing the structure of both the houses and delivered negative compliments to her father-in-law whom she had never seen in her life.

Raji's injuries were bleeding profusely. Only a psychologist could see and feel the intensity of her wounds. She felt frustrated on the fact that her *tantrik* spell could not stop the work. When she wanted it to remain half-constructed, the full-fledged house after all came into existence. Her jealousy and grudge against you grew stronger. She wished to reduce you into ashes but unfortunately she could not. And in the process her blood pressure went up so high that Prabhat had to be called for urgently. I don't know, what both had discussed, but Raji looked a bit relaxed after that. Perhaps Prabhat had suggested to her the ultimate strategy and it appealed to her.

On 20th October 1985, the *greha-prabhesh* function was

held. It was done very modestly rather as an inevitable ritual observed with minimum requirements. Including the two Brahmins we were hardly seven or so. You had urged father to invite Khuki, and her husband who was then visiting Orissa for the Durga puja. Pravas Babu a thorough gentleman understood every bit of the domestic politics. He did not like Sudha or Raji. He also hated Prabhat in spite of the resemblances that both the names might have had. He always adored our father because he was the only person who among other male members of the household approved of his marriage with Khuki, when he proposed in 1976. Father also had a strong liking for this gentleman who allowed his wife to work in Orissa and to visit him only during the long holidays. Father enthusiastically showed the new house to him, and Khuki recorded each and every incident that she thought was worth reporting to her mother and sister.

The function ended at around 1.30 p.m., and we reached Cuttack by 4.00 p.m. You two were left behind because you were expected to spend at least one night in the new house. I didn't tell you earlier because you might have felt disheartened but I heard very clearly Khuki and Raji discussing several unpleasant things about you and father. I was thoroughly convinced that Khuki was in Raji's camp : from the heart of her heart she was not our well -wisher.

It was February 23, 1986. Father was in his chamber since morning. At around 1.00 p.m. he had a bath, went to the temple and on his way back he again examined the patient who had just arrived from a remote area. God alone knows what Raji had added to the mutton curry. As soon as father had his lunch he felt a tremendous chest pain, and it was so severe that everything was over even before the doctor could arrive. Our innocent mother, you still had not realised that father had died. As soon as Dr. Bajoria rushed in you ran to fetch him from the gate, helped him examine father's pulse and heart. When he closed his brief case and went near the door you followed him asking for the prescription. "It was a case of heart attack," he replied! "What? What do you mean?" He looked at you sympathetically. You, perhaps, don't remember what happened to you next. You fainted there, briefly though.

We could not even imagine that Raji was slow-poisoning father. Perhaps, that day she had added a larger quantity and/or father's body had reached the limit of absorbing poisonous shocks. Little did we know otherwise we could have insisted on a post-mortem.

Raji was keen that the last rites should he accomplished at the earliest. She made all efforts to suppress her joy, yet it overflowed from her eyes, from her face, from her gait. As the reporters got the news, they started crowding in. Father was the only neurologist in Orissa till his death. Raji took all initiative explaining to everyone that it was a case of heart attack. The family was not prepared to face it. The crisis came all of a sudden and so on. When reporters wanted to talk to you, she made all possible efforts to stop them from meeting you. You were, of course, not in a position to talk to anyone. A person who almost looked hale and hearty in your eyes, disappeared in the air like a bubble. Unbelievable. Your mind could not accept it, you spent a few days almost in delirium. No one found you howling or shouting but the pain was inexplicable.

As they were making arrangements to take the body for cremation on 24th February at 4 p.m., you almost broke down. Aunt Bulu was a constant support to you I must say. When the news reached me and I arrived, both Sudha and Raji came closer to me almost pushing everyone. Sudha was trying her best to shed two drops of tears. "In my old age if I become immobile there remained no doctor to look after me," she said. As I tried to console her taking her into my arms, I felt retaliation. Perhaps she did it unconsciously because she needed no consolation. Raji just closed her eyes and folded the upper jaw of her ugly face to pretend pain. Tears were too cruel to her, they did not co-operate with her even when she prayed for them with all sincerity. The same response I experienced again, as I tried to take her into my arms she almost pushed me. After all feelings even in the sub-conscious mind do come out sometime or the other unknowingly, in spite of all alertness, that an individual may have cultivated to cover them. That is why sages always insisted on self-purification, which is nothing but working carefully to eliminate the evil thoughts from the root.

As soon as they departed carrying the body on the shoulders, Raji's laughter knew no limit. The pretext she gave was that the slum children fell down on the ice slabs, which were placed below the body to prevent its decomposition. Aunt Sibu could not tolerate it anymore. She exclaimed, "While someone's home is being ruined, someone else finds a reason to express her joy. Even an enemy would have a heart." Raji threw an arrow of fire towards aunt Sibu through her eyes.

Quickly father's signboard was removed, and the garage was rented out. I myself heard, Prabhat conspiring with Raji and Arun both, separately though. He insisted that Arun should not allow you to lock your room in case you decided to go away from Cuttack. He was aware that your brother, uncle Bapi, had offered you to stay in Nagpur. I had also suggested you to leave Cuttack and stay with me in Delhi. Bhubaneshwar home was not in your destiny and you could not have stayed there all by yourself. The neighbourhood was alien, it would not have been safe for you to stay there all by yourself.

As soon as the tenth day was over, your bangles were removed from your hands, and your vermilion was wiped out from the centre and forehead of your head. You were not allowed to wear colourful saris thereafter. Non-vegetarian food was out of question. Quickly Raji took out one of your brightest saris and wore it herself to tease you. She stole several of your saris in the past, which you ignored continually. She ordered for good fish curry to be prepared on the 13th day of father's last rite. She filled her plate with delicious food and sat right in front of you. She kept on praising the dishes; she wanted to generate greed in you. Everyone thinks others to be of his/her type only. Little did she know how much control you had on your mind. You remained calm, and kept consuming the boiled rice and green banana, specially prepared for you. Our society is unique. Along with the death of the man, the woman also ceases to exist if not in literal sense, for all practical purposes at least. Since *sati* is no more legal, the woman literally awaits death spending the rest of her life on minimum requirements. Ours was a slightly modern family; our grandmothers had not cut their hair off. So it could not be suggested to you either. But Raji was trying her best to reinforce the practice on you. Other aunts like Bulu and Meera put their foot down and opposed it. They also emphasised that you should keep eating fish. "The body', they said, 'is tuned/ used to a particular kind of diet. At this age a sudden change in the food habit may cause anaemia or other kinds of illnesses." But Raji and Sudha did not favour the suggestion. Aunt Bulu mumbled, "A piece of fish does not generate so much body heat in a fifty year old lady that she has to run for sex here and there." Sudha never liked aunt Bulu for her sharp tongue. Straightforwardness is a vice in the dictionary of the shrewd. Anyway, you did not allow the controversy to go on any longer. All you said, "The most precious thing of my life is gone; now do I have to debate to protect my food habits?" Raji's objective was to punish you, and you got it, she thought. She did not realise that your love for father was so enormous that nothing did your mind actually register. You could hardly make out the distinction between the food you were eating and what you used to eat when father was alive. The same was true about your clothes. Your attention was not on the earth; how could you make out the differences, and interpret that widowhood was a punishment, which was thrust on you by God as you had not been obedient to Raji and Sudha! The more she saw this state of mind of yours, the bitter she grew. She was disappointed that she had not been able to torture you. Once she told me, "Your mother is behaving like a country folk. She is an educated lady; it does not go with her personality that she keeps thinking about your father and does not come back to her senses." Yes, mother you looked as if you were intoxicated. The intoxication of pain had penetrated your mind. You had moved much above the daily requirements in life. I thanked God for this state of mind of yours. Pain itself is also a way to maturity and perfection. More than this I was pleased to note that the social customs and practices could not affect you adversely. The brighter side of pain was dominant in you. You proved to the world that love is the greatest of all. Parting from the loved ones leaves no scope for any other factor to be the cause of pain. I was happy to see you dismissing the thesis of our foolish society that widowhood is in reciprocity to bad conduct. Let people come and see how much father resided in your mind. Physical existence is only one dimension of a person. More important dimensions are to be discovered only when one physically ceases to exist. Immortality is something, which is related to these dimensions only : I felt like chanting these words day and night in front of Raji and Sudha.

Prabhat's instigations continued and Raji kept responding to them generously. For the next fifteen years you would have very bad times as per the prediction of Raji's *tantrik* : I heard her telling Sudha one evening. I almost fainted; "God! You still have many more things in store for mother," I murmured. Raji would utilise every opportunity to ruin you during this period, I thought. Bad times for someone are a period during which s(he) can be and should be pressed hard to a corner : this is what at least Raji believed sincerely. Instead of extending help to the affected soul one must try to take advantage of the situation in one's interest.

Prabhat made it clear to Raji that if you left Cuttack and went to live in Nagpur or with me, you should not be allowed to lock your bedroom in the Cuttack house. Two dimensions of the problem were highlighted if your room would be locked. First, you or your children would continue to have a claim over the paternal property. If the room remained unlocked, one day, very conveniently, they can refuse you entry into the house after removing your belongings. On the other hand, if your room remained under lock and key and they broke open the lock, they feared of a court case from your side. After all Prabhat was a lawyer. Secondly, their main purpose of having control over your belongings would remain unfulfilled if the room would remain locked. Your ornaments, your *saris* and all your fancy things, which you had accumulated over the years must be accessible to them. Borrowing Ramakrishna's diction

Raji, always commented, "We are free beings (*muktajeev*), others are (*baddhajeev*). I felt like telling her, "Your activities are indeed testimony to that." You stopped me saying so, "No need to react to useless words," you said. But I must say, I should have broken her head then and there. She would not have been left alive to torture you more in the future years. I would have gone to jail? I do not care. At least I would have had the satisfaction of eliminating some evil from my mother's life. You discouraged me to think on those lines, "God would do justice if we remain dedicated to him. We cannot take things in our hands." Yes, God would do justice but by then thousands of ages would pass! The exploited one would be left with his/her fossil to witness and receive that justice. God has better things to do. It is our illusion and misinterpretation of God's mind to think that he would intervene in our day-to-day affairs. What holds true at the aggregate level need not be true at the micro (household) level. People blame God for not helping them in their need. But my point is if you start with a wrong premise and you expect to get results of your choice, it is not the fault of God, it is the error of the human mind. I do not disbelieve in God but the interpretation of God oversimplified is a disservice rather than any solace to human civilisation. It makes people fatalist, escapist and idle. And for this, I entirely blame our cheap religious texts, which misguide people and prevent them from actually realising the signals that God offers in our day-to-day affairs, while He still continues to maintain clearly the domain of freedom or free will that He has bestowed on mankind.

In the mean time Raji started spreading that your association with the Rishi has brought all this misfortune to our family. She was scared that her conspiracy with her *tantrik* and the sudden death of father may draw the attention of the relatives and our well-wishers. In defence, she, therefore, became more offensive in criticising you : your minor faults if she could put up as highlights of the age, could act as a shield to conceal her vices. Grandma and Phuti supported her, "The Rishi has caused father's death." Uncle Arun, Nabu, aunt Khuki all believed them. We only looked at the statue of God shedding drops of tears; both loss of life and reputation we had to undergo.

Raji had a strong feeling that she could cause much more harm than what she could actually do if she could only succeed in breaking your faith in God. Her *tantrik* must have told her that your faith in God was reducing the intensity of evil she was carrying upon you. As an unsatisfied desire of her mind it took the form of prediction. She started demonstrating to the rest of the world that she had already attained a high stage of spiritualism. That state of mind prompted her to say that you had wronged, and you would, therefore, be punished. That punishment would come in the form of your paralysed body, loss of property and poverty, and the death of your children — all compelling you to be down in the street and beg until your death. All that she actually wanted you to undergo was put up in the form of predictions. If she would only succeed in actually implementing them by hook or by crook, people without knowing the actual cause of your misfortune would admire her prediction capacity and the strength of her spiritualism — 'the realisation of a pious lady'. Prabhat and Sudha were there to give a loud publicity to her achievements. She made her forecasts in my hearing range, and finding me indifferent, she called me and repeated those words over and over again. I almost uttered that that was exactly what she had been planning all these years. But God gave me the strength to hold my tongue. The inner voice, which I think, grew in me, without my knowledge, in the shadow of your teaching, whispered into my ears, 'No point in reacting to malice. Silence is golden'.

Your younger brother who came for father's last rites suggested that you should not be left behind in Cuttack anymore. If you could not come with me, then you must live with your brother's family in Nagpur. You were hesitant to come to Delhi because I was not settled by then; staying in a hostel, pursuing my studies. As soon as Prabhat came to know about your possible departure from Cuttack, he took Arun into confidence and impressed upon him not to allow you to leave Cuttack. Arun listened to him because he had self-interest. He realised that people in the neighbourhood would not spare him of criticism if they would find his brother's wife leaving the house within a month of the death of her husband. People would certainly believe that she was driven out of the house. To save his face he declared that you must not leave the house. I do not know if you heard it or not but I reiterated, "Who are you to dictate terms to my mother. She must feel free to decide what is good and bad for her. Given the state of her mind, her preferences must receive the top priority." Seeing my immediate reaction, he realised his mistake, and quickly offered an explanation, rationalising what he had just said, "No I was just thinking that she may like to live in the midst of her husband's belongings. That would comfort her greatly." I said, to myself "indeed," without of course moving my tongue.

Phuti and Nabu were engaged by Raji to scandalise me in all possible ways. They suggested to everyone under the strict instructions of Raji that my purpose of taking you away from Cuttack was mainly to extract what you were left with. My future wife would snatch away your ornaments, your money and the house in Bhubaneshwar too. Raji knew if everyone would tell you the same thing you might believe and decide to stay back in Cuttack and that would facilitate her plans to take tangible shapes. Subtlety is always stronger than the inscriptions. People tried to pollute your mind against your children but you faced it courageously. Your quietness expressed sumptuous indifference to the misgivings, and you won over the poison.

Next few years you spent your time partly with me and partly in Cuttack. Your sympathy for Sudha drove you to Cuttack most of the time. You always said, "Poor old lady! She had lost her mind under the spell of misinterpretation of facts and misgivings of her daughter. She does not know what she is doing. She has lost her most capable son. One day God would give her the realisation and then she would be able to feel the magnitude of her loss. We must sympathise with her."

Yes, mother, Jesus also said the same about those who put him on the cross. He prayed for them so that they might be forgiven, as ignorance had darkened their conscience with no scope for realising what they were doing. But do ever doers of wrong deeds realise what they do? Does God really give them any realisation some time or the other? Perhaps, yes. Otherwise men from every faith over the ages must not have thought so. Even if God does not exist, and God cannot give them any realisation, we who know that they wish harm to us can at least forgive them in the name of God and offer them kindness and love. And those who still cannot change even after receiving love in exchange of their jealousy need to be pitied. I took several gifts for Raji whenever I went to Cuttack so that she should never feel neglected. If she were married and her children would have shown her love, she perhaps would not have been so hideous. That is what I kept thinking. But my attitude did not have any positive impact on her. Altruism does not necessarily stop exploitation. On the contrary, it leaves ample scope for exploitation. Being guided by self-interest both the parties earn better outcomes than being altruistic. Altruism can pay only in the company of individuals with similar genes.

As Stark (1995) pointed out, it is good but not always does altruism result in improved outcome. At times an increase in altruism can make both the donor and the recipient worse off in spite of prompting enhanced transfers. Hence, mutual altruism also does not necessarily result in social harmony. This is because altruism can increase possibilities for exploitation and limit the availability of credible strategies, narrowing the range of possible beneficial social arrangements. That altruism does not eliminate conflict and that it can actually make everyone worse off, hence, leaving scope for exploitation and strategic behaviour, nudge individuals to vouch for commercialisation with self-interested behaviour.

Uncle Arun after observing me for several years did note that Raji was grossly wrong. He once commented also, "Even after so much respect shown to you, your attitude does not change to the slightest possible extent. It is a pity." I recall the short story by Khushvant Singh, "The Mark of Vishnu." I think it is safe to maintain a distance from those who are dangerous. Yes, in the beginning one must always have a positive approach to every individual s(he) comes across, and only after experience one may come to a conclusion. Once the intellect notes certain negative traits in an individual there is no need to show him/her love and affection any further. In self-defence one must avoid such individuals without, of course, paying them in similar terms, as Ramakrishna makes it very clear in *Kathamrita*. Unfortunately, neither father nor you understood it in your entire life span. If you don't listen to the God who resides in the coach, then your love for the God residing in the mad elephant can only prove to be fatal.

Another thing, which I often note in people, is a drastic change in their approach to the rest of the world after a couple of bad experiences. That is another extreme. If I had the misfortune of having unpleasant interactions with some in the past, what is the fault of the future? I cannot vent out my pent up emotions on all others whom I am yet to meet in life. I think merit lies in still holding a positive approach to the rest of the world even after undergoing filthy encounters. Successful are those who know and avoid the negative but hold on to positive.

After father's death I felt a bit hesitant to visit Cuttack. Even when you used to be around, and you repeatedly requested me to spend a few days in Cuttack with you, I would take a few hours to make up my mind. I felt as if I was a tress passer, though from legal point of view I was completely aware that I had every right to stay there. Somehow the polluted atmosphere always repelled me. Deliberately they would create more disturbances in my presence knowing fully well that I almost fainted in such circumstances. This was actually a strategic action. Without saying a word one can drive another out by pursuing what the other hates. However, the assumption is that (s)he is quite sensitive.

I learnt from our maid that Raji locked you up once inside the bathroom. The reason was that she did not want you to use that toilet, though it was constructed by father. She alone should have access to comforts. You kept screaming for an hour from the toilet. Then father's aunt heard you crying and came to your rescue. She advised you not to use it again. With your problem in the knee you decided to use the Indian style toilet. The main difficulty with this toilet was that it didn't have an attached washroom — the washroom was another 200 meters away from the toilet. Seeing your problem father had constructed the new one with all amenities. I thought, how mean people could be! Even when consumption of certain goods or services by one individual does not reduce that of the other, narrow mindedness can result in deprivation and suffering. But you again stopped me from retaliation. All you said was, "What is the point in blaming others. Had we not had such a bad destiny why would your father have to die so early, and why did we have to stay like guests in our own home?" I kept quiet then.

In some of my visits in 1994/1995 I felt uncle Arun had started looking much older than his age. His behaviour had also changed considerably. His actions and reactions were those of a eighty year old man. He complained of body ache, chest pain and so on. I thought, much of these problems were psychological than physical. His indifference to life had become increasingly evident. Otherwise he could have corrected some of the non-sense that was going around.

In the mean time I also felt that Arun's frictions with Raji were speeding up, particularly after Sudha's death in 1993. He saw his mother dying due to Raju's torture. Due to the old age as she became more and more dependent on others, Raju started ill-treating her. The same mother who supported her daughter all through her life in tormenting you had to literally die in the hands of her own daughter. As Raju found that her mobility was restricted due to Sudha'a dependence on her, she coolly pressed the throat of her mother one evening when others were not around. And the old lady passed away before her feeble body could raise an alarm. To the rest of the household it appeared as a normal death but the maid's little daughter had watched everything from the window. She conveyed it to many of us after a week or so.

Arun almost realised that all these years Raji had not been moving with a good intention. And the more he understood the more repentant he became for having supported her action all these years. Bitter his attitude became towards Raji. At some point he started hating her so much that I thought he would live no more. Repentance triggering off hatred for someone with whom one has to share the space under the same roof results in nothing but denial to life.

Raji also increasingly felt that uncle Arun was emerging as a strong opponent to her. She could not mix freely with Prabhat in public noting signs of resistance in the eyes of Arun. Of course, he never commented on her personal life. His main grievances against Raji were, I think, about her misbehaviour and an evil design that she carried in her mind, causing harm to whomsoever she disliked. He tried to change her several times in the name of the common Guru and the Lord. But it was to of no use.

Raji wanted to go out more frequently with Prabhat, wished to be dressed in the brightest of colours, with flowers on her hair-do and walking straight, smashing the heads of all her enemies, but she thought that the whole world was mocking at her. Arun became the victim of all this because the lack of an expected support to a person with a destructive attitude creates more intense revengeful attitude than what may emerge from the usual differences in views of the ordinary minds.

Soon Arun started looking pale. He even complained of a shadow following him day and night. Even if a rational mind would interpret this as an outcome of some psychological problem, at least I cannot rule out the possibility of Raji's involvement in slow poisoning uncle. She must have done it more frequently than what she did in the case of father, and given the age factor, uncle succumbed to his chest pain one night before good medical care could arrive.

As soon as uncle Arun passed away, the next in the queue was father's aunt to fall victim of Raji's wrath. A child widow, she lived in our house ever since her husband passed away. And in turn what has she not done for the entire household all thorough her life! Even for this Raji she used to get up early in the morning and prepare her breakfast, followed by all delicacies that she ordered for lunch and dinner. As Raji realised that she would become bed-ridden soon due to her old age, she decided to stop her medicine for blood pressure, and instructed the servant not to serve her food. Within a few days her condition grew worse, she could not watch her steps, fell down from the *verandah* one evening and succumbed to her injuries finally.

Nabu received a major setback after the death of Arun. He was relying heavily on uncle Arun for the maintenance of his family. Besides, he thought Arun would help him inherit the entire family property, and he would prepare all the papers for Nabu. The sudden demise of Arun disposed all his expectations. As a matter of last resort he decided to join hands with Raji. If he could drive you out of the house for good, then he could arrive at an understanding with Raji for the transfer of the property in his name. His intuition prompted him that Raji would be happy to receive a male support within the family, which could reduce her feeling of insecurity. In return she would allow him to pursue with his adventure for the illegal transfer of the property to his name.

Raji did understand the depth of Nabu's evil desire. But she was keen in short run gains. An important objective of her life, she thought, she would be able to fulfil if she could turn you out of the house with disgrace. Ever since your marriage she had imagined this. With no specific reason in the first sight, causeless malignancy one may call. She knew she would be able to handle Nabu later on. But if she would miss out Nabu's support this time, it would be impossible for her to see you being driven out of the house.

Both, for different reasons though, joined hands. They started spreading rumours that you had killed uncle Arun by taking recourse to *tantrik* means. The best way to escape a crime in this world is to place the blame on another individual before an iota of suspicion arises. Nabu knew the truth. But he could not afford to go against Raji keeping in view his self-interest. He supported Raji in all possible ways and danced to the tune that Raji played from time to time.

Several of our relatives were invited and a grand meeting was called urgently. The main theme of discussion was your inauspiciousness : your evil sight destroyed several stalwarts within the family, hence, you must be thrown out of the house at once. Nabu pleaded that if it was not implemented immediately your next strategy would be to kill him. You looked at every one desperately pleading your innocence. All of them put their heads down. Like Droupadi you ran from pillar to post for help but none came up in your support. The unanimous decision with the silent support of others that was arrived at was the doors of our paternal home would remain closed forever for you and us. I was communicated this decision through a telegram. I came quickly to take you back with me. Later you expressed your desire to reside in the

Bhubaneswar house and I acted accordingly a few months after.

I decided to write to some of our relatives at least challenging their action in extending silent support to Nabu and Raji. I unfolded intentions of both Nabu and Raji, and a large majority of our relatives did believe what I wrote. Some of them admitted their fault and asked for an apology. Though others did not write explicitly to be forgiven, they pretended innocence and ignorance of all complicacies. When ego does not allow repentance to arise, the latter takes the form of ignorance, pretended. I tried to forgive them all but Nabu and Raji.

Months later I met Nabu in a social function, and I decided to take it up with him. I asked him straight, "What makes you think that our mother has an evil sight, which has destroyed all the pillars of our home?" He kept quiet and repeatedly said that he did not know what he was doing. He was tremendously shocked by uncle Arun's death. I believed him and decided to close the matter there. However, I told him, "I believe in God. Sooner or later the truth will come out and you would, of course, know in the ocean of crimes who stands where." I am sure, he understood what I meant since his wife kept urging me to forget and forgive. I did not have the drive to pursue it further. But I did say that we did not seek the police support as it would have brought insurmountable disgrace to our family but in the ultimate court of justice, truth would prevail definitely.

Truth did come to prevail in a different form though. Initially Nabu's wife, Keya showed her deep concern for Raji, and Nabu also dutifully carried out Raji's orders. Three of them enjoyed the whole house. But all this could last only for a few months. Why? No one knows the reason exactly. I have only tried to gather facts from neighbours in bits and pieces and tried to analyse them for my consumption.

An important feature that emerges sharply in my analysis is that a home cannot stand on mere sand it requires hard rocks. Relationships based on self-interest are bound to break, as they cannot be hidden behind the garb of false concern for long. Mutual convenience was the only drive that encouraged them to stay together. As soon as it started evaporating, their follies became more and more prominent to each other. First of all, Raji felt Nabu was trying to grab everything. Nabu felt, Raji was dominating too much. Raji knew this but her point was, since she was contributing maximum for running the household she must have the ultimate say in every aspect. She should be the 'kartri' of the household. On the other hand, Nabu and his wife wanted her to stay as a guest in the household.

Soon interests clashed, and the Nabu *versus* Raji tug-of-war gained momentum. It took the shape of serious fights ultimately forcing the neighbourhood to intervene. Nabu by then had discovered all the secrets of Raji, her illegal and criminal activities to eliminate others. He kept threatening to disclose them to others. Raji, though she was also slightly disturbed by this, soon came to terms with it by posing threat in return to Nabu's life. She explicitly stated one evening when both the parties had almost come to physically assault each other, that she would get Nabu murdered by some of the criminal associates of Prabhat and Anil, Prabhat's elder brother, who had been a practising politician. Nabu was not all that shaken by this threat, as I was reported later by some of our relatives in the neighbourhood. He too took pride in having connections with some powerful characters in the society, who would least hesitate to commit a couple of murders. Raji grew little worried, realising the shortcomings of her threats. It ultimately struck her mind that she would expose Nabu's evil desire of grabbing the entire property. Nabu realised its serious implications and became more desperate. Both came down to the street seeking and mobilising support while scandalising each other in the filthiest language that the gospel of vocabulary could have ever offered in any age or time.

Raji wanted the keys of garage one day and Nabu was hesitant to pass them on. Ultimately when he was forced to surrender, he instructed the servant to insert them in her ass-hole. She in return showered on Nabu all possible adjectives and ill wishes that fate could ever usher in someone's life. Raji ultimately wished for Nabu's death caused by major accidents, disfigure of Nabu's face executed by the mercy of leprosy and finally, the untimely death of Nabu's seven year daughter and transformation of Nabu's wife into a notorious prostitute. God bless them! These are the people who visit religious institutions frequently. Whenever Raji stood on the dias to lecture on the life of Sri Sarada Devi, an epitome of sacrifice and simplicity, I always told myself the story of Dr. Jackal and Mr. Hyde. Such characters have always prevailed in our society; because of their duplicity in character they are less caught than their actual frequency. In these moments the instant reaction of the human mind, who at least had the misfortune of knowing all aspects of such characters, is to announce to one self, "How can God tolerate such things?" The next step is to declare, "There is no God, all this is based on false belief." But we forget to recall that aspect of God, which bears everything patiently. He witnessed the crucifixion of Jesus! He never descended to demonstrate miracles and stop what was being pursued on false charges. God does not have to unfold what is truth and what is wrong. Every action has an equal and opposite reaction : He believes in it and surrenders himself respectfully to that ultimate truth to define its course.

I once wrote to uncle Gyan, who lived in Banagalore, requesting him to intervene and bring back peace in the family. He wrote a very practical thing : "If three and a half persons cannot stay peacefully in that palace-like house no God can help them enjoy happiness." He was right — I have seen in poor households notwithstanding inadequate space for oneself and meagre amount to eat, joint families lived peacefully and enjoyed each other's company. But in our Cuttack house case they had no dearth of resources, only the lack of good feelings for each other.

Between the two parties, though one may be tempted to put both in one category, I would place a larger blame on Raji. And this is because she absolutely lacked adjustability, had a filthy mouth in addition to her selfish nature, rough temper and jealousy. Besides, she developed many more psychological problems : for example, she would not stand a couple sitting next to each other and chatting. Whenever Nabu's wife, Keya, wore a nice sari, Raji picked fault with her for some reason or the other and started scolding her. Keya's fault was that instead of ignoring some of the petty conflicts, she deliberately diverted her energies towards constructing them as important issues. Uncle Gyan advised her not to do this, particularly when he learnt that Nabu was developing some heart problem. But Keya did not take note of his advice seriously. Nabu, on the other hand, did not think intensely before reacting. And secondly, reactions to all incidents need not be of the same intensity. Certain things are to be ignored even after a hundred instigations; non-reaction itself is at times powerful in yielding desirable outcomes. Certain others are to be dealt with in terms of discussions leaving only a few incidents for arguments and no scope for brutal fights. But this is the philosophy followed by the civilians to keep the home going. In an uncivilised world it holds no meaning.

Nabu realised the importance of some of these facts of life but quite late. When the condition of his heart grew worse, he looked for an alternative, which seemed to him to be nothing other than leaving the house in Cuttack and staying elsewhere. He did it eventually and shifted to Calcutta. It was quite shocking to note that the property for the sake of which he did not want to leave any stone unturned, was given up by him instantly. If life would not exist, of what use would property be? Such a simple truth! Unfortunately man realises it only in the eleventh hour.

Keya came to know from Rosy aunty, a Christian lady who used to enter into trans after offering her prayers in the morning and evening that Raji has been involved with a *tantrik* invoking the support of a disastrous spirit. Once it strikes Nabu, he would be ruined given the condition of his heart. So Keya became determined on leaving Cuttack. Raji tried all means to stop them from shifting but they escaped avoiding all hindrances.

The fights of these two parties were ignited and accelerated by Phuti's unscrupulous politics and unending greed for money. She thought that all the money of uncle Arun was grabbed by Nabu, leaving nothing for her; hence, she must not leave the last chance. If Raji and Nabu would stay peacefully, obviously Raji would leave her money behind for Nabu's daughter. Phuti was, therefore, determined to ruin their relationship : she shared their feelings separately as a close friend of both the parties, and cross communicated the undesirable components in their most exaggerated and fabricated forms, suppressing the context and the positive views both might have had for each other. She was certain that she would be the immediate gainer of this fight. I tried to tell Raji about this, but she did not believe me.

Not for more than two years Nabu was alive after he left Cuttack. What a tragedy! He was the youngest of all brothers and sisters of our father and he died such an untimely death. I was in the US when I heard the news. I remember I sat dumb struck for almost an hour. The only thought that kept intriguing me was relating to the darker side of money; that can ruin families. Lamentation yields nothing, it is only an expression of helplessness. I hate to feel helpless. The next moment I made all efforts to overcome my agony. Nabu had insulted you and driven you out of the house, yet all my sympathies were for him. When I talked to you over the phone a day later, you also burst into tears. You thought not at that moment about the disgrace and humiliation he had brought to you in the past. You only recalled all his services that he had rendered to you or others over the years. In anger and hatred I cursed Raji and Phuti both. My inner spirit cried in pain. "If there is any God both will be punished severely," I told myself. The next moment I got back to my senses "No,' I told myself, 'our preaching does not endorse hatred. We must pray for our enemies too. Let God give them insight to realise what mistakes they have been committing. Every object, every living being is a manifestation of Brahman. We cannot afford to do harm to others. If someone has done so s(he) is ignorant but reply to ignorance is not thoughtless action." I discovered, I was uttering your words only. "God give me the strength to forgive them," I concluded.

Khuki was a constant support to Raji and Sudha, as I saw since my childhood. I thought it was natural to have an inclination towards her mother and sister. But, with what I was upset was her support for injustice while simultaneously she continued to show affection to us. But more surprised I was to note was Raji's indifference towards Khuki after uncle Arun's death. When she realised that she had used Khuki in all possible ways — Khuki extracting information from others' and thus enabling Raji to cause harm to others — she decided to chop off all contacts with her. She knew, if Khuki would not be allowed to enter the house, she would stop visiting Orissa, and finally, she would decide to have herself confined to Assam, at her in-laws place. Raji was scared : Khuki knew her secrets substantially while working as an agent for her, and Sudha had also divulged several things to Khuki as a matter of shared feelings. If Khuki would leave Orissa for good, Raji could afford to conceal all her activities, and pretend to be a religious lady. Given her oratory skills to offer discourses on spiritual leaders in India she would then spend the rest of her life with dignity and high social status. Respect and honour would usher in material comfort and thus she would have no difficulty in leading her life all by herself. Her spiritual image would attract so many individuals towards her that her loneliness would disappear into the thin air. All this is possible in India where ignorant souls have distorted the picture of spiritualism by all means. So Raji was not unrealistic in nursing her expectations. In fact she succeeded to a large extent to impress upon a significant number. People often appreciated her lectures saying how knowledgeable she was. She had a number of persons to serve her, to fetch her grocery and to help her with other work outside home. If she fell sick many were ready to stand by her. In this country in the name of religion anything can be achieved. Intellectuals lose their power of rationality. Even though they understand the truth at times they try to eliminate it from their mind thinking that it is the meanness of their mind, which is stopping them from experiencing the ultimate beauty hidden behind an ugly mask. But the truth is that it is not merely the musk, it is the face — the actual face, could be an ugly looking face too.

Raji and Phuti both celebrated the last rites of Nabu in Cuttack quite enthusiastically. Several Brahmins were fed and food was distributed to poor. I could identify two main reasons for this. The guilt feeling they had, prompted them to do so and second, to demonstrate to the society that they were deeply pained by Nabu's untimely death. Raji had the audacity to call you up and express her false grief, "Whose curse has fallen on our family? All the male members are passing away one after another untimely." You let a deep sigh come out of your heart — answered nothing. Why could not you tell her right away that it was all her curse, no one else's. But you are always determined not to speak unpleasant truth. You, a dead wood — and so am I in terms of patience and principle!

Though Raji was left to herself ever since Nabu and his family left Cuttack, Nabu's death brought her a relief, which let her enjoy the house and the cultivable land and it's produce with a monopoly right. Luxury if shared diminishes at an increasing rate, conversely when it is enjoyed alone, it inflates satisfaction manifold. Such was the psychology of Raji.

Phuti's visit to Raji paced up at an accelerated rate. Following the elder sisters strategy she also chopped off all contacts with Khuki. After the cyclone in Orissa Khuki went to see Phuti and her family. None came out after the maid opened the door. Khuki sat in the verandha for a while and made a loud announcement of her arrival and finally, departure finding no one turning up for almost half an hour. How much she had done for Phuti for last thirty years. The moment she would get her salary she would first meet Phuti and her children with bags full of gifts instead of thinking about her own requirements. During Durga puja she would buy the cheapest clothes for herself and present the most expensive ones to Phuti and her children. In return she never took anything from anyone. What Phuti did to her was perhaps her biggest gift in her life for which, she had waited all these years to receive in plenty. I was startled to see the behaviour of both the sons of Phuti. Did not they think for a while what Khuki had done for them? The elder one pretends to be a sensible chap. Was that an example of his sensibility? The younger one who himself was the father of an eight year old son could not realise the value of affection! Poor childless Khuki had to control her tears desperately before leaving their home. I don't blame Phuti's daughter-in-law. She is a new comer to the family, relatively speaking. She would follow what her husband and mother-in-law would instruct. If the mother was going crazy, both the sons should have tried to correct her. Instead they supported her greatly and to this Phuti took incredible amount of credit, "What obedient sons do I have!" Shame to her sons who do not have independent mind, who can not distinguish between right and wrong, who are as selfish and opportunist as their half educated mother.

Even for that matter Nabu did not do any less service to Phuti. I remember, after he had received his first salary, he got clothes for everyone. He presented the expensive ones to Phuti's sons and the ordinary ones to us. He never gave you a piece of thread in his life but he made it a point to offer a sari to Phuti during the pujas every year. As a younger brother I would say he did enough for Phuti and her sons. When Phuti's elder son went out of the country for the first time, Nabu gave his most expensive pullover to him. But he did not have the courtesy to return it to Nabu after coming back from Geneva. We might have had difference of opinion with Nabu on certain matters, he might not have been nice to you in certain occasions but that does not mean that we should ignore his good qualities. Phuti is ungrateful, as bad as a snake. That is why she could stab Nabu from the back when she knew that he had almost reached his last stages.

Her main allegation against Nabu was that his wife had criticised Phuti in front of her daughter-in-law. How does it matter if Nabu's wife commented on Phuti's character! Phuti herself never spared anyone. She was a living gadget of gossips : a nasty gossipmonger the earth ever produced, with malicious intentions. I realised the intensity of her malice the day I heard her abusing Nabu's wife : "I will make her a widow. I will make her sit on the street, I will reduce her to a prostitute, I'll see to it that she earns her livelihood from begging and selling her body." Phuti herself said so many bad things about the character of Nabu's wife. Phuti told unbelievable things about my character, I ignored them generously. This was the actual difference between her background and our background. It all reflected her immoral way of life about which she was extremely conscious, and by degrading others she derived a mental comfort. In her eyes, that is why, none in the world could bear a good moral character. Only she and her sons possessed all the virtues of the Heaven. And if anyone ever confronted her, as Khuki did, for saying nasty things about others, she became absolutely vindictive and proved to be more dangerous than a snake. What she did to Khuki was unforgivable.

Anyway God is there, as you always said. She would reap, as she would sow. By taking recourse to *tantrik* means, following the path of Raji, one cannot escape the fruits of one's evil actions. Time is immortal. It encapsulates the fruits of all good and bad actions. When one would get them is a bit uncertain to an ordinary mind, but their arrival is inevitable. As Tagore in one of his poems said that nothing is lost :

"Amaro anagata amaro anahato
Tomaro veena tare bagiche tara"

Well he said it in the context of a positive action. But if it holds for a positive act, it would hold for a negative act as well.

You decided to stay in Bhubaneshwar house and I had to leave you there though I did not appreciate it from my heart. At the back of my mind I had a fear that Raji would somehow try to harm you as she would come to know that you were staying there. But you did not listen to me. So things had to be worked out as you desired. In the servant quarter one family was brought in and they kindly agreed to look after you.

Days passed by. The world is too small a place. Raji saw you in the Ramakrishna Mission a couple of times and learnt that you were residing in father's house. She pretended to be concerned and tried to befriend you. Once or twice you avoided her but she succeeded in her subsequent trials. Shame on you! You never learnt from your thirty years' experience. Whenever I tried to caution you, you said one must not hate anyone. Fine, I did not ask you to hate anyone. All I wanted was that you should be careful about your enemies in self-defence. There is no point in becoming a foolish devotee. As I mentioned above, if you read *Kathamrita*, it is very clearly mentioned that you must keep a safe distance from dangerous people though you need not think of causing harm to them. But the biggest drawback of your character is whatever you think to be right can never be wrong. You pretended as if you were carefully following my advice but you actually did not. And you knew to the best of your knowledge that you would not follow them in future too.

Raji befriended you and started visiting you every now and then. You thought she was trying to take care of you as you were staying all by yourself. Ma, if she were so concerned she would not have had a connivance with Nabu to drive you out of the house. Whenever I told you this, you said, 'No, that she did because both she and Nabu were after the property.' Now that she knows we are not interested in that property and we left the house instantly, "her concern is genuine." Genuine indeed!

Raji brought food for you a couple of times and you consumed them readily. In the pretext of *prasada* she managed to stuff your stomach with whatever she wanted, and you followed her instructions like a mesmerised person. The lady residing in the servant quarter spoke to me over the phone that Raji had left some vermilion and some turmeric near a plant behind your bedroom when she visited you in one afternoon. When I wanted to check with you, you avoided the topic and asked me to ignore the unscientific things. Yes, Ma, I do admit many of these *tantrik* things are unscientific, and we cannot prove them logically. But my argument is even if it is baseless, when I know that someone is not my well-wisher, why should I take any chance with him?

Raji succeeded in convincing you that Nabu actually drove you out of the house, and that she was absolutely faultless. But I swear on God, Raji was the actual culprit. She motivated Nabu to actually implement it. Though Nabu might have had such a desire at the back of his mind he could not have thought of actually executing it. It is she who used Nabu's weakness for property to settle all scores with you. And she also knew that she would eliminate Nabu as soon as her objective was fulfilled, so that, the basket of gold falls into her lap unasked, and she would relish the chicken soup without taking the pain of cooking it.

Even every swamiji in the Ramakrishna Mission knew that Nabu misbehaved with Raji grossly and left the house after plundering the wealth. She in a way tried to infuriate you by saying that some of your marriage utensils and other stuff were looted by Nabu. You kept grumbling to me that Nabu did such injustice — things with which you had sentiments attached, must not have been wasted in this manner. But, Ma, why did you believe Raji? Do you think she was speaking the truth. What is the guarantee that she herself did not distribute your stuff to others in order to buy fame, and later put the blame on Nabu? She was just looking for an ally after she drove away Nabu from the house. Secondly, she was scared that you might go back to Cuttack one day to collect your things lying behind. So before she was caught, she wanted to inform you that most of your treasure were missing and passed on the blame on Nabu. Raji, who kept stealing you expensive 'saris' ever since we were children how could not she have done the same in your absence. Greed is irresistible, and it grows enormous when unchallenged.

The climax was approaching : perhaps you were fated to be so. That is why you did not learn from the past experience. In front of destiny, intelligence or action or carefulness or knowledge is nothing. It changes everything in its favour and the victory is ultimately of the destiny. Even God surrenders to destiny; all He can do is to raise his devotees' strength to stand up to the power of destiny and face it. Raji's constant and continuous effort to make you suffer and to declare to the whole world that you were a sinner and that was why you suffered so much was in rapid progress. If she would survive you and that too with full vigour and vitality, the impact of her words would be more effective and demonstrative. Moreover, if she could manage to acquire an important status in the society by offering regular discourses on religion and spiritualism, her words and views on you would outweigh all that is truth, all that we call moral, all that is factually correct. Dishonesty in the garb of spiritualism is even stronger than the almighty Himself.

I asked you continuously not to visit the Cuttack house anymore though you told me over the phone that you wanted to get your ornaments and 'saris' from the cupboard for my marriage. You did not listen to me, and one afternoon you decided to go yourself in a taxi. As soon as Raji came to know the purpose of your visit, she could not resist herself. The moment you collected your treasure and were about to step down the staircase she pushed you down with all her strength.

As such your feet had grown weak after suffering the pain of arthritis for so many years. Mentally also you had lost strength after encountering tragedies in life. You could not maintain the balance and rolled down the staircase. However, you managed to get up and walk up to the taxi but fainted as soon as you were in. Your maid called me in the evening to deliver the message that you were brought home unconscious. However, you came to your senses after a couple of hours, but complained of severe pain in the right leg. I came to Bhubaneshwar in a couple of days time. Your condition had grown worse. You had become absolutely bed ridden. The x-ray report showed a major fracture and the doctor recommended for an immediate surgery.

The operation was carried out. Unknowingly Didi informed Raji about the recent developments. What a big mistake you did by not telling us the actual reason of your fracture. We all thought it to be a spontaneous fracture caused by your illness.

Raji came to see you in the hospital when you were lying unconscious following the surgery. As you were coming back to senses, you were almost dying in pain. What a pleasure it was for Raji! Her face was beaming. She expressed the joy of winning all the three worlds! Sometimes you were chanting the name of Ramakrishna in your semi-conscious stage. Raji looked a little pale. She was jealous to note your spiritual progress. "She might recover," she said very softly. I knew she wanted you to die so I was not very much surprised by her statement. I only wished that you had told me what she had done to you. I would have left no stone unturned to hand her over to the police.

Raji offered to take Didi's children to Ramakrishna Mission in the evening. Her joy knew no bound as I found when I went to collect them after two hours or so. Swamiji had apparently told her, "Your grand children are very bright and modest — a rare combination of qualities. After all they are your grand children!" This is what she always wanted. People should never come to know about her misconduct and miscreants. The society must admire and worship her as the most knowledgeable, devoted and pious lady. Achievements in our life notwithstanding her evil desires and ill-wish, must be attributed to her potentialities and supreme power. If you would die, she would remain as the sole survivor among the elders to take the entire credit of whatever any of us may attain. That is what she always wanted : to push you aside to the dark room and prove that she was the only blessed soul.

I admire her courage in retrospect. She did not even feel frightened for once that you might tell what she had done to you when you went to collect your belongings in Cuttack. She was so confident. She was perfect in acting. A confident criminal can murder anyone on the earth and in all probability would remain unnoticed. Most of our dos and don'ts have been forcefully related to outcomes, good and bad, so that we do not execute our wishes by impulse. The intelligent criminals know this truth and, therefore, they learn to overcome fear. And any act, good or bad, performed fearlessly assures perfection and complete success. Idealists also talk of fearlessness but returns to a positive action are only marginal whereas criminals have more substantive and tangible returns at least in the short run to realise the effectiveness of their action. Raji believed this because she was successful in almost all her missions of negative action. Success in one prompted the other, and it went on endlessly with confidence begetting confidence.

You developed several complications immediately after the surgery. Your blood count was only 6 though the medical report prior to the operation indicated it to be 12. Not much precaution was taken, and subsequently your condition deteriorated day by day. You were required to get drip, blood and oxygen.

One evening I was away for an hour or two from the hospital. The doctor wanted me to get some injections from the market. The lady attendant we had engaged for the day had already left and the other attendant had not arrived yet. The nurses were as usual engaged in continuous gossip. I requested them to keep a watch on you, though I knew, none of them would take the trouble of going all the way to the first floor when hot gossip was on over a cup of tea and *pakoda* in the duty room in the ground floor. Still I requested some of them and mentioned that I would be back in an hour or so.

It seems someone was keeping a detailed account of my movement in the hospital. As soon as I had left someone walked into your cabin and removed the oxygen pipe, the blood needle and the drip. The last attempt to end your life!

I don't know why I am recalling all this today and trying to pen them down bit by bit. It appears to me like a moment of eternity. One fraction of a second but it seems to contain the whole history of your life, several lives — lives which have gone unnoticed, uncared, misunderstood and wrongly interpreted depending upon how powerful the criminal survivors have been. Millions of women in our country have suffered this and have been buried in the grave of shame, dishonour and filth. They have been crushed between the wheels of injustice and dishonesty. Perhaps their souls have found a voice in me after their long struggle. They have ignited my consciousness. The whole night I am awake, my eyelids had forgotten to drop. Voices travel from the unknown land to speak to me, speak desperately their unheard words. They all are alive even after dying thousands of death imposed upon them by the society they lived in. Their spirits live all around the sky, they have all come down the ladder to speak to me from the bottom of their heart. They have found me as their platform.

My flight is early in the morning. I must get ready. The Asian Productivity Organisation invited me to their conference on status of women, and I have been wondering all these days what to speak. Now I think I have got the materials, and they are substantive enough for my paper and policy recommendation. I will definitely not forget to say, it is better to be exploited in the job market than to be exploited at home. We are just beginning to sow. This much price we can afford I am sure.

* * *

Mother, the woman who lived in my heart has arisen, awakened. The voices of several millions suppressed over the centuries and exploited in all possible ways have taken shape in me. I stand today on the dais as convener for seven countries to narrate the problems that women face in these countries. God give me the strength to speak the truth. Give me the power to express the misery I have been made to encounter in my life through many other lives. This is my earnest prayer to you lord, let me do justice to my role. Let my voice represent those unheard ones.

I will not stop in my mission. I have stood on the dais not for my sake, it is to tell the international audience the problems of those underprivileged, and exploited ones. Let all my existence be transcended to theirs, let my soul speak their language. Yes, the woman who dwelt in me has awakened. The woman, who is expected to be seated on a lion and receive the worship of the universe, has wept in the dungeon over the centuries, and today she has opened her mouth tearing off all the hurdles of inhibition.

You do exist, mother, you do exist. You exist to read my letter. Your form of existence has only changed. The girl children of today — the future generation — in whom you find your eternal existence, look forward to living peacefully and joyously in their happy future home. That day is not very far off. The mission is already on motion. The positive outcomes of your suffering are going to bloom soon like a bunch of lotus emerging from the filth. I am sure, you would read all my contents and carry them to your eternity.

The glow of the setting sun absorbs and carries your worries to the sea of darkness, and in darkness the stars share your misery and carry it to the vast ocean of light. You arise again to give yourself selflessly. You are beyond the harassments of your in-laws. They cannot touch even the wheels of the chariot you are riding on. Raji had your effigy burnt in the burial ground wishing you an early death but eternity is beyond the evil forces of *tantra*. Raji detached one head from your effigy but you are gifted with life that is endless. You are manifested in the entire universe, you are holding the whole cosmos in your manifestation. Physical existence is only one of the multi-dimensional existence that eternity holds. You are one in many, you are many in one. End does not exist for you because you have no beginning either. I bow to your unlimited spread :

इंद्रियाणामधिष्ठात्रीभूतानांचाखिलेषुया ।
भूतेषुसततंतस्यैव्याप्त्यैदेव्यैनमोनमः ।।

"*Endrianaam adhishthathri*
Bhutananchakhileshu ya
Bhutesu satatam tasyae
Byapti devyae namo nama"

(Presiding over the senses of all beings
and pervading all existence,
to the omnipresent Goddess,
who individualises creation,
we bow, we bow.)

(*Durga Saptasati Chandi*, Chapter V, Canto 77)

affectionately,
Your Son

